Paperback ISBN: 978-1-7382608-7-4
eBook ISBN: : 978-1-7382608-6-7
Audio ISBN: : 978-1-7382608-8-1
Hardcover ISBN: : 978-1-7382608-9-8

Wolf Pine Publishing
Ontario, Canada

For my girls -

Samantha and Andrea

I love you more than all the stars
in the universe.

May you never stop dreaming. xo

PERILOUS PINS

A Sydney Jones Mystery

Book #1

Grace Bowen

Wolf Pine Publishing House

Chapter 1

"Woo hoo! Another strike for Mike!" Sandra Watt cheered. "You're up next, Sydney!" she called, sitting in front of the big display above our lane that showed our scores. Sandra was dishing out her usual words of encouragement and direction in generous helpings. I picked up the ball hesitantly. Thank goodness they were the small balls, not those giant ones with holes for fingers. Although I always thought those could break a finger, I had never seen one up close. I was pretty sure I couldn't handle those. I was already having a hard enough time and still questioning my sanity since joining the weekly bowling league. Harry could be persuasive.

My first two balls ended up in the gutter. My third knocked down all but one pin. I wondered how the machine swooped down at just the right time to reset the pins for the next player. Bob, the manager, occasionally had to walk down the alley to the area behind the pins where all the machinery was. If something got messed up, he'd go back there. Last week, George offered to help, but Bob stopped him, saying it was dangerous and that he didn't want customers getting hurt. His words immediately sparked my curiosity, and I wanted to see what it was really like back there. I couldn't help myself. All I really knew about the pin setting machines was from what I had seen in movies, and I wasn't sure how accurate that was or if it applied to all bowling alleys. To find out more about five-pin bowling pin setting machines, I made a mental note to look them up. I had always been curious and overly inquisitive. I suppose it was just part of my nature. As a kid, my mom always warned me, "Sydney, you just mind your own business, young lady!" she'd say. "How many times do I have to remind you that curiosity killed the cat?" I thought it was strange she said that all the time, especially since we never even had a cat. Now, here I was, in my mid-forties, still overly curious, and still hearing my mother's voice echoing in my head.

"That's great Sydney. You almost got them all." Sandra's smile was contagious and despite my mixed feelings about joining this league upon Harry's urging, I couldn't help but like Sandra. "George, you're up next."

We called ourselves the Wildcats. Not sure why, but most of the team had been bowling in the same league for a few years now. Ever since, the new owners fixed the place up. One side was all the bowling lanes. There were seven of them. The other side was a pub with live music every Saturday night. It was usually busy, but that didn't surprise me, because so far, I had seen little else in the way of bars anywhere close to Blueberry Falls. I had only ever bowled a handful of times in my whole life, so I am not sure how Harry convinced me that this was something I should do. He said, "You will love it, Syd, and it's a great way to meet people. You've been here since spring, and I bet you haven't made any new friends yet". It was true, I had barely met anyone since I had moved in – well, except for the customers I met at Angela's Bookshop, where I worked three days a week, but I just hadn't had a chance yet. "Too busy," I kept telling Harry. "Oh baloney! You barely leave your house. You'd still be cooped up in your house," Harry said, "if it weren't for our morning coffee chats and occasional lunch visits to Sally's." Harry could argue with the best of them and he called me out on everything. A straight shooter is how I would describe him. And occasionally, a cranky old man. Although he was only seventy-two, I think. I appreciated his honesty and knew it was his way of showing he cared. His calling me out was one reason I liked him so much. Held me accountable. Well, that, and his knack for brewing the best coffee I have ever had.

"Sydney, you're up". Already? Ugh. Here goes nothing, I thought, as I rolled three gutter balls in a row.

"Not to worry. It's only your second week. The rest of us have been bowling for a long time. You will improve every week, I'm sure." Sandra touched me hesitantly on the shoulder. "We are all going to grab some wings and a drink after the game. You should come too."

"Oh, I don't know. I've got to work in the morning."

"We don't stay very late. Most of us must work tomorrow too. Besides, Riverbowl usually closes by 10pm on weekdays."

***

We were all gathered around a big wooden table in the corner by the pool table. The pub area was separate from the bowling alley, although there were no walls dividing the two sections. When you first walked through the double oak doors - which I thought added a ton to the character of the place–you landed in a small cozy foyer equipped with coat racks and benches for the customers. Riverbowl had a unique vibe, which was apparent from the moment you arrived, and a genuine feeling of warmth and community which I had never experienced in the city. It reminded me of "Cheers", that 80s television show starring Ted Danson. I loved that show. The place lived up to their motto, which was stamped on all their merchandise, "You Belong Here", and I thought it couldn't be more appropriate.

Dan and Haleigh Masterson, a local couple, owned the business. They had three young children and were loved by almost everyone in Blueberry Falls. The first time I met them was a couple of months ago, and I immediately liked them. They were charming and made me feel like I belonged, even though I had only moved to Blueberry Falls the month prior. Harry, my retired neighbor, had taken me out for my birthday that night to watch the live music, which was a Saturday night regular occurrence. People packed the place. The band was fantastic. I thoroughly enjoyed myself, despite my earlier reluctance to celebrate, as I was planning to sit at home feeling sorry for myself. Harry had hoped to see his old buddy Bob, the manager at Riverbowl, but Dan said he had called in sick at the last minute. They both agreed that Bob was rarely sick, and missing work was unusual behaviour for him. While Dan and Harry chatted, I wandered around to get a closer look at some sports memorabilia. The sign out front announced Riverbowl as having Northern Ontario's largest sports memorabilia collection, and as my eyes scanned the walls and shelves, I could not disagree. There was a glass cabinet against the wall across from the bar that held a collection worthy of a sports museum placement. Since my birthday night, Harry and I had gone regularly on Saturday nights to watch the live talent and have a beer. We usually only stayed about an hour or so, as Harry claimed he needed to get to bed earlier now that he was seventy-two. I didn't mind, as I had never been a night person and was usually up and moving before dawn. An old habit I had still not broken.

The pub section was on the north end of the building, separated by a long bar. I sat sandwiched between Ellen Caldwell and Sandra Watt, waiting for my order of honey garlic wings. Ellen had ordered the same thing. She bowled with the Thursday night league too, and although she wasn't on my team, we were already friends. I had first met Ellen when Harry and I were watching a folk music duo at one of Riverbowl's live Saturday nights. She sat with us most of the night with her friend Josie. Bob, the manager, also tried to sit down with us to chat with Harry, but he kept having to get up and help behind the bar whenever another group arrived. Bob had known Harry for many years. They used to be neighbors until Harry moved. Bob used to be the manager at the local hardware store until he had quit suddenly one day. Harry said Bob and his boss often clashed, and he wasn't surprised. One day, it all came to a head, when Bob and the store owner Ed Hall had a big blowup and Bob quit, storming out of the office in a fit of rage. That was over five years ago, and Harry said he had no idea what the argument was about, but assumed it had something to do with differing management approaches. Bob had big ideas about changing the place up to make it more modern, and Ed wouldn't agree to those changes because he liked it as it had always been, so they argued. Shortly after that, Bob got a job as the manager at Riverbowl. And since Dan and Haleigh were younger and more open to changing things up, there weren't the same issues. Harry also said that Bob was now far less of a hothead than during his younger days, and he was surprised Bob had lasted as long as he did at the hardware store. Despite being friends, Harry knew Bob had a short fuse and didn't always work well with others. Harry was the exception. They had been next-door neighbors for many years and had always got along famously.

Ellen Caldwell was around my age and looked like she could have been a model in her younger days. Beautiful long brown hair and large dark brown eyes. She had an exotic look about her that made me wonder about her heritage. Mesmerizing. Her personality matched her beauty. She was such a lovely person, and we hit it off right away and exchanged phone numbers that night with promises to get together for coffee soon. Aside from Harry, Ellen was fast becoming one of my first real new friends in Blueberry Falls. Josie, the lady that came in with Ellen, was a little harder to get to know. She seemed to know everyone in the pub and spent most of her time wandering around to different tables to drink and chat with her friends.

Our food orders arrived, and George raised his beer. "Cheers! And welcome to the team Sydney. We are so glad you joined us this season," George continued. Everyone followed suit and raised their glasses to say welcome. Even the bowlers from the other teams that had joined our table after the game, and everyone had turned to look at me.

I could feel the heat rising into my cheeks, burning from the attention. "Thanks everyone." I mumbled. I felt Sandra's gentle elbow nudge as she leaned over and whispered, "I am so happy you joined the Wildcats, Sydney. It's nice to have another female on the team." She winked. "I bet you will throw lots of strikes in no time at all and show all those men up." Sandra winked. Her smile was so warm and genuine, I couldn't help but relax a little, which was an enormous achievement these days when in a large group of people.

This season, The Wildcats team comprised Sandra and me, plus four men, George, Mike, Marty and Bill. There were six teams in total for the Thursday night bowling league, and each team had six players. Harry was supposed to be on our team but had to drop out just before the season began, because of a lingering shoulder injury that had flared up. Originally, I had agreed to join the bowling league because Harry had said I didn't get out enough, which was true, but I only agreed to join because I assumed he would be playing, too. Harry had apologized for having to drop out, but after his shoulder flare up, he would have to sit out for at least part of the season. Marty, a man who was also new to town, took Harry's spot at the last minute. Like me, Marty didn't know many people yet and kept to himself. He was a quiet, tall and awkward looking man, with wide rimmed glasses that sat on the end of his enormous nose. I guessed him to be in his mid forties, even though the brightly colored jacket he wore looked like something that might have been worn by one of the Beatles back in the 60s or 70s. George said we were lucky to have him join because without a sixth, we wouldn't be able to participate. George was the organizer of The Wildcats and liked to take charge whenever he could. Harry told me George ran the town gossip line and warned me to be careful about what I said around him because it would spread around town before sunset that day. George was married, but his wife was on The Alley Cats team. She was much quieter than her husband from what I had seen so far. Mike Marshall was our youngest team member. He had worked with his dad for the local township since graduating high school. His parents were Frank and Nancy Marshall. They bowled too, but were on The Grizzly Bears team.

There were five teams besides The Wildcats in the Thursday night league. The Grizzly Bears, The Alley Cats, The Hot Dogs, The Cougars, and The Pink Ladies. The Pink Ladies all wore matching bright pink outfits each week. They were comprised of six local women that were all apparently young mothers, happy to be part of a group that could get out once a week without their kids, husbands, or any other family obligations. They were a rather loud group of women, and I found them quite funny and entertaining. I think they simply enjoyed the freedom of a night out. All the other bowlers seemed to adore them. In fact, many had seen them grow up. Small town life was sure different from what I was used to, but it was growing on me; slowly. After the first night of team bowling, I told Harry that The Pink Ladies were a hoot, and it made me think of my old friend Natalie and me in our younger days. So much fun. Natalie Coleman had lived on the same street as me in Barrie for almost twenty years. I had been making weekly day trips there for visits with Nat, and shopping, of course, but I really missed our daily walks and talks. I was trying to adjust to my new life in Blueberry Falls, but I missed my friend and my old life. The day trips helped, and I knew I would eventually meet more people here and hopefully be able to settle into my new life, but I'm not going to lie. I was having a hard time.

"Would you like another drink?" I hadn't noticed the server come up behind me.

"No thanks. I have to drive, so I'm good." I said. I watched as Ellen Caldwell got up from the table and walked away. She appeared tipsy. She had a tiny frame, and I would bet that only a couple of drinks could throw her off. Ellen played on The Alley Cats with Sara-Lynn Mitchell, Alan and Ruth Gainer, and Mike Marshall's parents, Frank and Nancy. My wings arrived and I must admit, they were delicious. In fact, all the food and service were excellent. For a small-town pub, this place was great. Laughter erupted again from the other end of the room. Everyone was laughing at one of George's jokes.

Once everyone got their orders, things seemed to quiet down as everyone got busy eating their meals. I was happily chowing down mine, but heard raised voices coming from around the corner. As my usual nosey self, I wanted to check it out. Ellen hadn't come back yet from the washroom, and I wanted to make sure she was okay. As I neared the corner, I could tell the voices were coming from Bob's office. One sounded like Bob's, and the other was a woman's voicc that sounded like Ellen, but since the person was crying, it was hard to be sure. I stopped and waited, unsure whether to continue walking past Bob's office or just wait. Next, I heard a door slam, and the argument was over. I heard footsteps heading away from me, so I rounded the corner, planning to pretend I was totally unaware of anything. As I passed Bob's office, I glanced in and could see him through the door window. He was sitting at his desk, looking at his computer. I walked into the ladies' washroom just as Ellen was coming out. We almost bumped into each other. Her eyes were slightly red, but she smiled at me and mumbled something about seeing me back at the table, then walked on past like nothing had happened. Well, whatever it was about, I guess Ellen didn't want to say anything. It wasn't any of my business, anyway. I didn't even know her very well.

When I returned to the table, Ellen was putting her jacket on. "I'm heading out now, Syd. I think I better call a cab, though, because I might have had one too many to drive." As soon as she said it, Marty piped up.

"I'll drive you home Ellen. I don't mind." Marty volunteered. But Ellen shook her head no.

"It's fine. I want to call a cab. You stay here." But Marty continued.

"No, I'll drive you home. Taking a cab is wasteful. Just give me a minute to pay my bill." Marty insisted. Ellen looked uncomfortable, and she didn't appear to want a ride from Marty. She just kept shaking her head no.

So, I stood up and whispered. "Ellen, I'm leaving now, anyway. Why don't you let me drive you home? I can bring you back tomorrow before work to pick up your car." Ellen smiled and nodded a hearty yes.

Ellen turned to Marty. "I'm fine. I'm going home with Ellen, so no need to worry." I watched as Marty sat back in his chair and simply grunted his response. He really was a strange duck. The drive home was fairly quiet. Ellen mainly stared out her window, occasionally pointing me in the right direction to get to her house, which wasn't far from mine or the alley.

"Thanks for saving me tonight. Marty can get a little pushy sometimes. I think he means well, but I hardly know the man, so I didn't want him driving me home and getting the wrong idea. You know what I mean?"

"Yep, I totally get it. See you next week Ellen. Tonight was fun."

Chapter 2

The ringing jolted me back. I carefully set the photo back in the box and quickly swiped the back of my hand across my wet cheek. I wasn't ready yet. Unpacking these last few boxes would have to wait a bit. Maybe tomorrow. Relieved for the interruption, I picked up my phone. "Hey Nat! So glad you called. Saved me from the dreaded task of unpacking the rest of my stuff."

"Aww, that's hard I bet Syd." I swear Natalie could read my mind sometimes and always seemed to know what to say. She was a loyal friend. "I wanted to check in on you 'cause I haven't heard yet about your game night. Do any better than last week?" I had mentioned to Natalie that Harry had talked me into joining a bowling league and how my first night was a complete disaster. I had almost quit on the spot. Nat had convinced me to give it another try first.

"Ha. Ha. Nat. It was okay, I guess. I think I did better than the first week, but that's not saying much. I still had a lot of gutter balls. If it wasn't for Sandra's encouragement, though, I would probably have quit already. She's so sweet. You would love her, Nat."

"Well, I can't wait to meet her then." Natalie said. "Aside from the gutter balls, did it go okay? I mean, did you chat more with anyone or get to know more people?"

In my mind, my most embarrassing bowling moment replayed. I had one shot where my ball actually ended up in the next aisle over. I shook my head to erase the ridiculous image. Sweet Sandra had assured me that others before me had committed similar crimes. I was not the first. But the glares from the neighboring team still stung.

"Yes, I met a few people. I'm sure I will get to know them all much better after a few more weeks of bowling. If I don't die of embarrassment first from all my gutter balls." I laughed.

"Of course you will, Syd. You are usually great at meeting new people. Give it time." Natalie Porthouse and I had been close friends for almost twenty years, and I missed her terribly. From the day Natalie and her family moved into my neighborhood, we hit it off. Natalie and her husband, Greg, were wonderful additions to our aging neighborhood. I wish I could have stayed there, but everything changed once I learned about my ex-husband's affair. Gerard and I split up, and I simply couldn't afford to remain in the family home by myself. It broke my heart to leave, but I needed to move forward. I knew Greg Porthouse had stayed friends with my ex after we separated and I couldn't fault him for that, but Nat had been so loyal to me afterwards and I couldn't help but feel glad that she decided she wanted nothing to do with Gerard since then.

"Greg went out for drinks last weekend with Gerard and his ridiculous new girlfriend, Martha. I swear that woman is just plain evil. Breaking up your family the way she did. I told Greg I had a headache and wanted to stay home to rest to get out of it. I have no desire to spend even one minute with her, or Gerard, for that matter."

Despite my gratitude for Natalie's loyalty, I knew she would eventually have to talk to Gerard, as her husband was his best friend. But for now, I was still hurting from having lost my marriage, home and daily contact with my best friend, among so many other things. Like my confidence, for one. But here I was, in my new home, still surviving, despite the betrayal and upheaval. Harry kept telling me it would soon get better, and I really hoped he was right. As it was now, I felt like I had become a bit of a recluse, which was not like me at all. Natalie had previously voiced her concern about my change in behaviour since the divorce, and even more so, since I had moved to Blueberry Falls. "You really ought to get out and meet people, Syd. It's no good staying at home in that lovely little house of yours all the time. And don't bother trying to tell me I am wrong because last time I visited, I chatted with your wonderful neighbor Harry, and he filled me in about it." I had already heard this lecture before from Harry. That was how I got roped in to joining the bowling league. The only way I could get Harry off my back. Usually, Harry played in the league too, but his shoulder had been acting up so much, he decided he better sit this season out.

"You used to be out all the time, going here and there and doing all sorts of fun things." Oops, Natalie was still going on and I had half zoned her out.

"I am trying Nat. Promise. Besides, you didn't let me tell you about last night after the game. We all got together for wings and beer, and it was interesting."

"Interesting? Like what? Give me all the info, girlfriend. I am in total withdrawal without our daily walks and chats. I miss you like crazy, you know. And I don't mean to get on your case all the time. I just miss the old Syd, and I miss our old life together."

"First of all, I figured out that George, one of the older guys on our team, is a real gossip. Pretty sure he would talk about anybody if they weren't within hearing distance. Not sure how much of what he says is true, but I learned a few things about some of the other teams. Nothing Earth shattering yet, though." I happily talked to Natalie about all the different bowling league members I had met so far, and I was feeling so much better already. Just having a good chat with Natalie was what I needed most right now. "We were all having fun and laughing about the game and eating our wings when I heard shouting and noticed that Ellen, she's one of the players on our team, hadn't come back yet from the washroom for so I went and check on her. She had been a little tipsy walking away. Well, anyway, that's when it got a bit interesting."

"Go on." Natalie urged. "What got interesting?"

"I was coming around the corner towards the washrooms and I heard people arguing in the manager's office. The door was closed, so I couldn't say for sure, but it sounded like Bob, he's the alley manager, and Ellen. She was crying, and he was telling her to calm down. I heard the door opening, so I jumped back around the corner and heard footsteps leaving the office. It sounded like they were going to the washrooms, so I followed. As I walked past Bob's office, I didn't even look that way. I didn't want him to think I had overheard anything. And I decided it wasn't a good time to inquire about working there on weekends to pick up some extra cash. I will go and see him another day though, because I could really use the extra money."

"Ya, that was probably a good choice. Maybe wait for a better day to ask about a job. I wonder what the argument was about. And what the crying was all about." Sometimes Natalie was just as curious as me about things that probably weren't any of our business. Yet she was always calling me nosy. "Did you say anything?" Nat added.

"What was I going to say, Nat?"

"Ya, I suppose there wasn't much you could say without looking really nosy or inconsiderate or something."

"Right. Maybe it's a normal thing around here. Who knows?" But something in my gut told me it wasn't just nothing. And even though it wasn't any of my business, it piqued my curiosity.

The rest of our conversation mainly focused on my new house furnishings and my job at Angela's Bookshop. And how I needed to pick up some more work hours soon. "I wish we could talk more, Nat, but I've really got to get ready for work now. I'm trying to get there a bit earlier today. Angela said she has an appointment she needed to get to this afternoon."

Chapter 3

As soon as I walked into work, the intoxicating aroma of books hit me, and I took a deep breath to experience more. To me, the mere smell of a book could calm me. There's nothing else like it. Funny how certain smells can just do that. Magic. Old books especially have the very best smells and Angela's Bookshop had an entire section devoted to old books that she had collected during her travels. The books in that section were ones she had collected and were often rare editions and hence not books that I could afford to buy, so I felt lucky just to be able to hold them, feel them, read them, smell them. There were cozy, oversized chairs placed strategically all around the store. Angela's Bookshop had the quaintest little reading nooks waiting to be discovered throughout the store. At the back, there was a larger sitting area where the monthly book club would gather to discuss their chosen read and a little area complete with coffee, tea and snacks. Angela figured a customer would be more likely to buy a book if they had to walk all the way through the store to get their coffee. I thought it was a brilliant idea, and it sure seemed to work.

The front of the store had two enormous windows that let all the light in. On one side of the door was the check-out counter. The other side housed the bestsellers of the month. About half-way back, there was a small set of three stairs that went up to where the large sitting area was. This was where the old books lived. Right beside them was a full shelf dedicated to books about the area and the books by local authors. We had several authors from the Highland District, which was where Blueberry Falls was located. Apparently, small town life inspired the creatives.

After taking in another deep breath, I felt ready to start my workday. "Good morning, Angela." I smiled as I walked behind the counter to hang up my jacket. I set the bag from Sally's on the counter. "Harry and I just had brunch, and the blueberry turnovers were delicious. I thought you might like one too." Angela was the sweetest person ever. I guessed her to be in her early seventies, but I was never any good at guessing people's age, so could not be sure. She was so warm, inviting and soft-spoken, and she brought out the softer side of me – not a side I showed to many, just by being her own sweet self.

"Oh, thank you, my dear. I love Sally's turnovers. Especially the blueberry ones." The town was named for the massive fields of blueberries that grew abundantly in the area. Angela gently placed the bag in her purse. "I will take this with me and eat it on the road. Are you good if I leave now? I should be back before four and I can help you close up the shop." Angela lived in the apartment above the bookshop. We closed at four on Saturdays and the shop wasn't open at all on Sundays.

"Of course! I don't think it will be that busy now. The summer holidays are over and most of the tourists and cottagers have gone home." Angela had offered no information about where she was going, just that she had an appointment and didn't want to be late. I didn't ask, which was unusual for me because I was overly curious, even when it really wasn't any of my business.

With her hand already on the door handle, Angela turned. "I forgot to ask, are you planning to come to the book club meeting on Tuesday night? I could use your help if you are available." The book club had been running for almost twenty years apparently and was Angela's favorite event at the shop. It ran the third Tuesday of every month, from September to April. May was a busy time in Blueberry Falls, with locals preparing for full gear before the tourist season officially began.

"Absolutely. I was planning on coming anyway, but I will be early and help you set up."

***

It was almost three before there was finally a lull. The first part of the afternoon had been non-stop customers. I headed to the back to make a tea. I was hoping to get a few minutes down time, but before I could sit, I heard the doorbells jingle, so I headed back up to the front.

The man was tall and handsome - in a rugged way - with just the right amount of stubble. Not that I had any interest in men right now. He stood looking at the best seller rack, but as I approached, he looked up at me and smiled. Good God! That smile. I couldn't help but smile back. My big goofy smile. Ugh. What was wrong with me? As I approached, I caught a whiff of cologne, although I don't know what it was. Not Old Spice. My dad wore that, and it was not like that. I inhaled a little deeper. The smell sent a slow feeling of heat down the back of my neck, right down to my knees. Oh boy. Get yourself together, Syd. "Hi. Can I help you find something? I'm Sydney and I work here. I haven't seen you in here before, although I must admit, I have only worked here for a few months now." What on earth was I babbling on about?

"Good to meet you, Sydney. I'm Matt. I haven't been in the shop all summer. My summer work hours are longer, and unfortunately, I can't find time for reading. Today, I'm looking for a gift for my niece, Katie. She's turning fifteen and is, thankfully, a book lover. Different from many teenagers these days, I think." His voice was smooth and deep, and I didn't know why that even mattered to me, but I thought it sounded like one of those narrator voices they sometimes have in movies, like James Earl Jones or Morgan Freeman. Mesmerizing.

"Do you know what books she likes to read? We have a lot of young adult choices over here." I pointed towards the YA section.

"She likes mystery books. Joanne told me she just finished that Good Girl's Guide to Murder series." I nodded. Maybe Joanne was his wife. Matt continued. "Joanne is my sister. Katie's mother." He offered.

"Oh, I've read that series. It was good. Over here there are some other series similar that she would probably like. They are good." Matt followed me to the teen mystery section of the store. I picked up the latest in the new Melanie Bolton Mystery Series and handed it to him. "Do you know if she has read any of these yet? So far, the first five of the series is out."

"I will take a chance and get all five." Matt filled his arm with the five books and headed for the checkout. "Thanks for your help. I bet she will love these." At the checkout, I wondered if Matt was single. I wondered why I would even care. I wasn't interested in dating anyone. My divorce still felt fresh, even though we had parted ways almost two years ago. I had a hard time accepting my single status. Even worse. My divorced status. Two years was barely any time at all compared to the twenty-plus years of marriage to Gerard before he…….

"Well, thanks for your help." Matt took the bag of books from my hand. "Maybe I'll see you here again soon. Or maybe at the Tuesday book club meeting? I try to get to them when work allows."

"Yes, I'll be at the meetings most times, I think." I started to ask him where he worked, but before I was able, he had already gone through the door. I finally had time to sit and enjoy my tea before the next customer arrived. It had been a busy afternoon, and an interesting one, I thought, as my mind wandered back to Matt. I picked up the mystery I was reading between customers and almost made it to the end of a chapter before I heard the doorbells again.

Angela struggled through the door as she was carrying a large grocery bag in one hand and some old books in the other. I rushed over to hold the door open for her. She said nothing until after setting everything on the counter and hurriedly throwing her coat over the rack, but I could just tell she was itching to tell me something.

"You wouldn't believe what I've got Sydney! I'm just thrilled to bits I could talk Frank Harmon into selling these books to me he found in his father's attic. Look at them! They are in perfect condition. It's unbelievable. And he barely wanted anything at all for them. He said they didn't really mean much to him anyway because he wasn't a book lover. Frank said he was more interested in his father's '59 Chevy parked in the garage." Angela unloaded her arms with her bag, a handful of mail items, and the books. She spread the books out across the counter for me to see. "Mark Twain first editions of Tom Sawyer, The Prince and the Pauper, and Huckleberry Finn. Aren't they wonderful? Perfect condition." Angela beamed with pride at her rare find. As I flipped through the pages, Angela busied herself with unpacking her bag and going through the mail. Along with collecting books, Angela loved to buy different herbal teas and make them in her store for her customers to try while they searched for the perfect book to buy.

"Oh, here is my bake-off entry reminder. I completely forgot that was coming up. Not much time to get the entry form in. I have never missed a year since I took over the bookshop from my father." Angela placed the form on the counter for me to read. "All the businesses along Main Street compete in a bake-off competition at the Blueberry Falls Autumn Fair. It's actually really fun, and the winner gets a great big trophy to display and bragging rights for an entire year. Such a shame I will be away this year for my lovely grand niece's wedding that weekend. I am happy to go to the wedding but disappointed that my bookshop won't be represented. Such a shame." Angela went back to unpacking her new tea selection, looking a little less excited than just moments before. "Didn't you say you used to bake all the time when Posh was younger?"

"Yes, I said that, but that was just my daughter and me baking for fun. Although I did used to bake with my grandma lots when I was young. And she used to enter all the fairs with her pies and cakes. She was a fantastic baker." Images of standing on a chair at the counter with my grandma flooded my mind, and I couldn't help but smile. They were wonderful memories from long ago. Angela had brightened once again, as she looked at me, grinning.

"You could take my place Sydney! You could represent the bookshop this year, so we wouldn't miss out. What do you say?" Angela beamed at me with hope. How could I say no now?

"I guess I could, but I haven't baked in ages. I don't even know what I would make to enter, and I don't think I have any of the needed ingredients in my kitchen yet. But it certainly would be a good reason to dust off grandma's old recipe book and test some of her cakes and pies out." Angela's excitement was contagious. Next thing I knew, I had committed to enter the bake-off at the Blueberry Falls Fair to represent Angela's Bookshop. Oh boy. What had I got myself into?

Chapter 4

"That coffee smells so good this morning." I mumbled with a mouth full of fresh blueberry scone that Harry had made at who knows what hour this morning. I took a deep breath to inhale the aroma of coffee beans wafting through Harry's kitchen while I waited.

"Didn't sleep good again?" Harry asked.

"Not really. My mind was too busy going over my expenses again and again. I need to get more hours at the bookstore or pick up some hours elsewhere, I think. It's been challenging, I must admit, adjusting to my new budget." Just the thought of having to budget for everything now was stressful.

"I haven't had to worry much about expenses for a long time, once Gerard's business took off. In fact, I rarely thought much about money at all during my marriage. Except when we were first married. Then, we watched our spending closely. I must admit, the last few years spoiled me. Money wise anyway. Although Gerard was never around much because he was always working."

Harry handed me a big mug of steaming hot coffee. I wrapped my hands tight around the mug and took a cautious sip, so I didn't burn my tongue. Ahhhh, just what I needed. I still had not got used to the idea of living alone. I bought my little bungalow right after our divorce was finalized because I knew I needed a fresh start. Posh was all grown up and graduated from university, and now she had just got a great job in Ottawa. I was very proud of my daughter and happy that she had found work right after graduating, but I wish she lived closer to home. Ottawa was over five hours away, so we could no longer just meet up for a quick visit. I suppose I would just have to drive there and visit as often as I could. My new job would complicate that a little, but I was sure Angela would give me the time off when I wanted. I think the real issue was that I hadn't got used to my new status as a divorced woman with a grown child that no longer needed me. I was feeling a little sorry for myself, and I knew I had to give myself a kick in the rear and smarten up. But frankly, I had never imagined myself as being anything other than the wife of Gerard Jones and Posh's mom. Gerard obviously had other plans, and they didn't include me. Instead, they included a much younger woman than me. All those years down the drain and here I was, in my neighbor's kitchen, feeling sorry for myself. I was in my mid forties, in a new town, with a new job, and no friends, except for Harry, of course.

Harry refilled my cup. "Did you ask Bob yet about getting some extra hours at the bowling alley? Weekends at the pub are busy, especially when they have their live bands playing."

"I was going to ask him last Thursday after our league bowling, but he was in his office most of the night with his door shut, and then he had that argument with Ellen, so I decided I would wait for another time." I had already filled Harry in previously about the argument I had overheard at the bowling alley.

"I wouldn't worry much about Bob and Ellen arguing. They've been friends for years and I'm sure they will sort it out. Besides, Bob is a hothead and argues with lots of people. It usually passes over pretty quick with Bob. You did say you had been a server before, right?"

"Ya, I did, but that was ages ago. I haven't worked as a server in such a long time. I'm not sure I could remember how to make all the different drinks." While I couldn't imagine myself working in a bar again, I was open to trying if the manager hired me. What I did remember, was the fantastic tips I often got from the customers.

"Tell you what. How 'bout I take you over there today after my physio appointment? Sonya is still working on fixing this damned shoulder of mine that keeps flaring up." Harry rubbed his right shoulder absently as he spoke about it. "The alley opens at noon and Bob is usually there by late morning, sorting out deliveries and paperwork and such. I can pick you up around eleven." I nodded in agreement, and we sat in silence, just enjoying our coffees and scones for the next while, until Harry jumped up and said he had to get to his appointment.

"Thanks for my morning wake up Harry. I'll see you in a bit." I called out behind me as I headed out the door to my own house, which was right next door. Buying a house next to Harry Lufkin turned out to be incredibly lucky. He was a real gem.

***

We pulled up in front of the alley. There were already two other vehicles parked in front. Harry pointed out the big old Buick as Bob's. "I don't know why Bob is still driving that big old boat. It is a gas guzzler." Harry shook his head as he parked his car.

"It reminds me of the car my dad used to drive when I was a kid. We could fit five of us across the giant back seat if we squished in tight. It was a convertible, and my dad just loved driving that boat all over town." It was surprising how quickly my memories came flooding back as vivid images danced in my mind. Shiny mag wheels and sharp looking chrome. "Every Saturday in summer, my dad would be outside washing and waxing that car. Every week, until the weather turned cold, he'd follow this funny ritual, then park his precious car in the garage, covered, for winter. And God forbid I ever got my bicycle anywhere near it when getting it out of the garage because he thought I might scratch his precious car. Sometimes, I wondered if he loved that car more than us."

"I remember saying something like that to Bob once. I think I said he seemed to love his car more than his wife, and he just laughed and said, *well, it's possible.*" We were still sitting in Harry's car in front of Riverbowl when I noticed a big black pickup truck pull out from behind the alley, which was weird, because there wasn't any parking back there, just a narrow dirt laneway they used sometimes when unloading supplies or building materials. I only knew that because Haleigh took me through the back door one day to show me their new dock they had just built. Riverbowl was in a fantastic location, as the property backed onto the Magnetawan River and gave Dan and Haleigh Masterson private access to the water. I squinted my eyes as I looked at the truck, but it didn't help. I still couldn't make out the driver, but was pretty sure it was a male.

"Hey Harry, whose truck is that?" Harry tried to turn to where I pointed, but the truck was already pulling out of the parking lot and headed towards town.

"Hard to tell. I just got a quick glance. Plus, every other person around Blueberry Falls drives a pickup. What make was it?"

"Pretty sure it was a Ford, but not positive. They were gone before I really got a good look. I just thought it was weird that someone was back behind the alley. I thought Dan and Haleigh drove a white Dodge."

"Maybe someone was dropping something off for them." Harry dismissed my questions and grabbed his door handle. "Come on, girl. Let's go chat with Bob and see about getting you some work."

The place was quiet, which was understandable, since it didn't open until noon on Mondays, and it was shortly after eleven when we arrived. They apparently ran a senior's league on Monday afternoons, which comprised a small group of elderly Blueberry Falls residents, who all lived at the retirement home just outside of town. Other than that, Mondays were apparently quiet, and they were only open until six. Harry said Bob often sat at the enormous desk doing paperwork, but when I peeked into Bob's office, it was empty.

"Not in here." I called out to Harry, who was checking behind the bar. I walked into his office to have a better look around. Maybe that was the nosey side of me emerging. A half-full pot of coffee sat on the credenza behind his desk, and the light remained on. A large file cabinet and a coat tree rack sat in the back corner on one side, and the other corner housed a large green leafed plant of some kind that I couldn't identify, mind you, I couldn't identify most types of house plants. Having a green thumb is not a phrase one would use to describe me. I had more of a black thumb. Bob's desk was bare except for a few items. A silver name plaque sat on the front of his desk with the name, Bob Filmore, Manager, engraved in bold letters, announcing his title at Riverbowl. There was a pile of papers stacked neatly on one corner and two coffee mugs. One mug had cars printed on it and it held a bunch of Riverbowl pens. The other mug was black with the "You Belong Here" stamped on the side. I walked over and saw that it was almost full. Picking up the mug, I noticed it was still warm.

"He must be around here somewhere, Harry. His mug is full of coffee and it's still warm." A brown fall jacket lay over the back of the office chair, which I assumed belonged to Bob. I checked the pub area next. "Not out here either."

"Maybe he's out back unloading supplies. That could explain the black truck we just saw." I followed Harry past the pool table to the back door, which sat partially open. "Hmmm," Harry mumbled as his brow wrinkled under his hat. "He must be out here, or he would have locked the door." Harry and I walked out back where there was a small dumpster, a partially completed patio area, and a dock. Along the back wall of the building lay a neat pile of lumber and other construction materials, likely waiting to be used to finish the patio. I had only ever been back here once when Haleigh showed me the new dock they had put in. It was a pretty cool little spot. "I hope they finish the patio soon so we can sit outside and look over the river while having our beers. That would be a bonus." I took a quick scan around the area. "It doesn't look like he's out here, Harry. But I can see fresh tire tracks, so someone has been here recently. I doubt the tracks would have stood up to that downpour we had last night, so my guess is that they are from that truck we saw pulling out a few minutes ago." Harry nodded his head in agreement as he searched further down the laneway, while calling out Bob's name.

"He's not here, but he can't be far, because he wouldn't leave the door open. Likely had his hands full. You go check the washrooms, and I'll look behind the lanes." Harry pulled the door shut behind us and we headed past the bar and towards the other end of the building where the bowling area was. Harry took off to check behind the lanes. I turned left to check the washrooms and almost crashed right into Ellen, who had come rushing around the corner. I skidded to a stop just before impact.

"Oh Sydney! You startled me. I didn't realize anyone else was here." She had black smudged makeup under her eyes, and she looked like she had been crying.

"We just got here. We're looking for Bob."

"We?"

"Oh sorry. Harry and me. He's gone back behind the lanes to find him."

"I've been looking for him, too. I thought maybe he was down here by the washrooms, but he's not." Ellen pulled her sweater tight across her front, as if trying to ward off a chill, although I found it quite warm myself. "He asked me to meet him here, but I can't find him anywhere."

"Hey Bob!" Harry's voice echoed through the empty lanes. "You back there?" Harry was already halfway down the side of lane one, which led to the pin setting machinery. "Bob, you back here?" Harry repeated his calls to Bob. Ellen and I hastened to catch up to Harry, who had almost reached the bottom of a set of stairs. I had never noticed them before, but you couldn't really see them from the other end where we bowled from. The process of resetting pins was a mystery to me, and I was eager to learn how it worked. I remembered Bob's previous warnings to George about the dangers. I'll be cautious, I noted to myself.

Memorabilia filled every inch of space along both outside lane walls. All autographed, I believe. The collection was like nothing I had ever seen before. I mean, this place had more charm and charisma than that famous restaurant dedicated to Mickey Mantle in New York's Central Park where we had visited during a family vacation a few years back. What I knew now that I didn't know then was not anything I'd ever imagined. Looking back, I could now see that even then Gerard had distanced himself from me. He was even a little distant from Posh, our daughter, which really used to bother me. I kept thinking I had angered him, but his answer was always, "No, not you. Just lots on my mind." The Mickey Mantle Restaurant reportedly housed over three hundred individual pieces of sports memorabilia, including a plaque honoring "The Mick", which had originally hung at Yankee Stadium's Monument Park. I preferred the sports memorabilia collection at Riverbowl, combined with the cozy atmosphere of the place, to Mickey Mantle's Restaurant, but I was probably biased since this was now my home base.

We all stood bunched together at the bottom of the stairs. Bob had not responded to Harry and now we questioned whether we should even go up, but it was becoming concerning that he was nowhere to be found by any of us. Harry went up the steps to the platform first. We tagged closely behind. At the top, there was a long platform spanning across the entire back side of the alley, as it ran behind all the lanes, just above the pin setters. I looked down at the machinery which was running even though there was no one bowling. It fascinated me. Apparently, I am easily amused. Harry was a few lanes ahead of us when he stopped abruptly. He turned and held his hand up, relaying he wanted us to stop walking forward. We were just passing the second lane and Harry had reached lane four. I looked where Harry was staring. There, at lane four, lay Bob's limp body. Ellen screamed, and I automatically turned to shield her from the awful sight. She had already turned pale and was shaking. I immediately looked around for some kind of emergency stop button or switch. I was sure there had to be one somewhere. Or at least an on/off switch or plug of some kind. I was frantically searching. My brain screamed at me. "How the heck do you stop this thing?" Finally, I spotted it. There, on the wall by lane one, was a large red button, with large red lettering above it stating, PRESS IN FOR EMERGENCY STOP. I hit it hard, hoping I was not making things worse. The machinery all came to an abrupt halt.

"You need to go back, Ellen. Get off the platform." I am not sure how I stayed so composed, but it wasn't the first time I had happened upon a dead body, unfortunately. "It's not safe and you might fall." She was frantic, and I worried she might pass out from the shock. I left Harry and started walking Ellen back towards the stairs, dialing 911 at the same time. Glancing back, I saw Harry bent down, checking his friend for a pulse. It seemed clear to me that Bob was, in fact, dead by the state of his body, but I'm no doctor. Slowly, Harry shook his head back and forth. No. I relayed the information to the 911 operator. The 911 operator informed me they had dispatched EMS, ambulance, and police, and that they were on their way to Riverbowl. I turned my attention back to Ellen and had to physically set her hand on the rail. She gripped it tightly, and I hoped her legs would not buckle. "Sit down on the step Ellen." She complied. She looked really pale. Even her lips looked white, and I thought she was going to faint at any second. It was understandable, especially if she had never seen a dead body before. And I knew she and Bob had been friends for many years, despite the disagreement I overheard between them the other night.

I thought about the last time I had found a dead body, a couple of years back now. I had happened upon the body accidentally while walking down a trail with my dog one evening. But that wasn't something I needed my mind going to right now. Right now, I needed to make sure Ellen was okay, and I also had to check on Harry, who was still standing over his friend's body in lane four. I could hear sirens approaching from a distance. They slowly got louder. "Will you be okay sitting here for a minute, Ellen?" She nodded her head up and down. Her hand still gripped the railing, and her knuckles were white from how tight she was holding on. "I'm just going to talk to Harry right over there." I pointed towards Harry, but she didn't even look up.

Walking back along the platform, I was much more aware of my surroundings. Although I had never been back there before, I scanned for anything that I thought might be out of place. An old habit I picked up a few years ago when I had been helping a friend solve a crime. But that's another story for a different day. There was a patch of oil spilled near where Bob lay dead. Could he have somehow slipped on it, then hit his head? Had he been trying to reach a pin that had fallen? I saw nothing that looked out of place, but I really had no idea. Then I spotted a cup of Tim Horton's coffee sitting on the ledge. Automatically, I picked it up, but quickly set it back down again. The cup was still warm and felt almost full. Crap! Had I just contaminated evidence? I noticed Harry watching me.

"Try not to touch anything else," He instructed. Harry had been a homicide cop for over half of his police career. When I first moved to Blueberry Falls, he had told me all about it. Seven years into retirement, I could tell he still missed his job. He said sitting around his house all day bored him to tears. Shortly after retirement, Harry had started a handyman service to keep himself busy, but last year, he had stopped doing it. He explained that seventy-two was too old to be crawling up on people's roofs to fix their gutters, along with many other jobs that had become increasingly difficult as he aged.

"Bob was always so careful back here, Syd." He stood up and walked over to where I was standing on the platform.

"That coffee cup is still warm and almost full. I know I shouldn't have touched it, but I didn't figure it was fresh. Don't you think that is weird, since he had a mug of coffee on his desk already?" Harry nodded yes. "If Bob's coffee was back in his office, then whose is this one? I thought Bob didn't let anyone back here because it was too dangerous?"

Harry studied the back shelf where the cup sat. "Ya, it's weird. He wouldn't come back here to have coffee with someone. And you're right, Bob never let people back here. He didn't even want Haleigh back here after he started as their manager. He was always telling her it was his job now to do the pins maintenance. Harry shook his head back and forth. "Something just doesn't feel right. I was a cop for almost forty years, and twenty of that I was in homicide division, before I retired. Something is off here and I'm not so sure it was an accident." Harry's voice was so quiet, I had to lean in to hear him. "Do me a favor and don't touch anything else, okay? And don't say anything to anyone either. Except the detectives that are going to question you, of course."

"All right, Harry. I won't." I put my hand on my friend's shoulder. Finding his friend's body visibly shook him, yet he remained composed. I supposed that being a detective for all those years had taught him that. Both of us looked around at the area near lane four while we waited for the police to arrive. We were looking for anything that would reveal how Bob had died. I pulled out my phone and snapped a few photos of the scene, but quickly slipped it back into my pocket when I heard voices approaching. I turned towards the stairs where Ellen still sat with her head leaning against the wall at the side of the stairs.

Three uniformed officers came rushing up the stairs and onto the platform. The fourth one, a female officer, stopped beside Ellen and started asking her questions. I watched for a moment, but the officer didn't seem to get much of a response from Ellen. As the other officers approached, Harry stepped forward and began describing how we had found Bob, then called 911. The platform became quickly overcrowded, and I wanted to get off, but couldn't get past everyone. The officer at the back started giving instructions. "Okay everyone. I need you all to clear this platform. This is a crime scene and there are too many people here." The two cops in front of me turned and sidled past the one in charge. Harry followed them. "Ma'am, I need you to go down the stairs and wait. Detective Franklin will question you in a moment." He stepped to the back of the platform to allow me to pass.

Looking up, I was surprised to see Matt, the man I had met at Angela's Bookshop the other day. I had no idea he was a cop. The look on his face told me he was just as surprised as I was to see me here.

"Oh, I didn't realize it was you. Sydney, isn't it?" All I could do was nod my head up and down as I tried to pass him on the narrow platform. As I inched along, I caught a whiff of his cologne. It was that same intoxicating scent as he wore at the bookstore the first time we met. I didn't know what it was, but I really liked it. I looked down at the narrow space I had to get by Matt. I was afraid of falling. He grabbed my arm and helped me pass by him.

"Don't worry. I won't let you fall." No words would come out as I navigated along the platform. I just kept nodding. By the time I reached the stairs, someone had taken Ellen to sit on a bench at the front of the alley. My hands had started to shake. I think shock was setting in as I walked along the edge of the laneway towards the waiting officers.

I sat on a bench in silence. Harry sat beside me. Ellen was across from us, sitting with the female detective. I hadn't noticed earlier, but there were also paramedics in the alley. One of them came over to me and handed me and Harry a water bottle each. "That must have been quite a shock finding a body like you did. Do you mind if we check you both over while you sit here, just to make sure you are okay?" After being checked over, the detectives questioned us and then told we could leave. Harry decided it was best to drive Ellen home as she was still in no state to drive. So the three of us left Riverbowl and sat in complete silence all the way home. Each of us lost in our own thoughts after the day's turn of events.

After dropping off Ellen, Harry and I went to his place for a coffee. We both sat at the kitchen table waiting for it to brew in silence. I just sat and listened to the gurgling, and Harry stared out the window. Today had been a shock, and we both needed time to process the earlier events. By the time I was on my second cup, I felt ready to speak. "We need to find out who was in that black pickup truck. Are you sure you don't recognize it?"

"I don't. But I only caught a quick glance, and I really wasn't thinking much about it at the time. Had I known how important it was, I might have done better." Harry admonished himself. "Maybe it means something important. Or maybe it was just a truck dropping something off for the alley. Hopefully, Matt and the other detectives will investigate it. I mentioned it to them during questioning."

I took a long slow sip from my mug before I said any more. "Do you really think Bob's death isn't an accident? I mean, it looked dangerous back there on that narrow platform, and I can see why Bob didn't want any customers back there."

"My gut tells me there is something more to this, Syd. I don't think it was an accident. And I need to know what happened to my friend." We both fell silent again while we finished our drinks. It had certainly been a hard day, and I just wanted to go home and have a long hot bath. I gave Harry a hug before I left. He was still staring out his window.

Chapter 5

The morning after we found Bob's body in the back of the bowling alley, Harry called to ask if I would accompany him to visit Victoria Filmore, Bob's wife. The short drive over to pay our respects to Bob's widow was glum. Victoria and Bob Filmore had been close friends of Harry's for a long time and Harry was shaken up about the death. I didn't know what to say to make him feel better, so I just stared out his car window and watched the scenery, while holding a fruit tray on my lap that we had picked up on the way. "Can't very well go in empty-handed." Harry said.

Harry pulled his car up beside the curb in front of Bob and Victoria's gray brick bungalow. The long double wide driveway was full of vehicles already. Likely close friends and family that had come to comfort and support Victoria through her grief of losing her husband of fifteen years.

"I didn't know they were selling their house." Harry said as he studied the HOUSE FOR SALE sign displayed on the front lawn. "When I sold my house to buy the one I am in now, Bob said he would never move from here because he loved the neighborhood so much. We were neighbors for a dozen years. That's my old house right there." Harry pointed to the red brick house beside Bob's. Both houses had attached garages and large lawns. I could see why Bob wouldn't want to leave here. We stood on the sidewalk looking at the two houses. This was one part of town that had a sidewalk, as many streets in Blueberry Falls didn't have any. Harry stood quietly with slumped shoulders.

I gently laid my hand on his arm. "This must be hard for you, Harry. All the memories you two must have shared. And yesterday. Finding your friend's body like that. I am so sorry. This whole thing is awful." I just wanted to give Harry a big, long hug, but I knew he wouldn't appreciate that right now. He was trying to stay composed, and a show of softness could make it worse. I knew it would for me anyway, and I bet Harry felt the same. Harry squared his shoulders, and despite his seventy-two years and the toll of losing Bob, I could see his inner strength come to the forefront. I thought about all the terrible things he must have witnessed over the many years he spent as a detective. Things far worse than what we saw yesterday. But finding your longtime friend's lifeless body had taken a visible toll on my dear friend.

Harry took a deep breath. "Okay. Let's go in and pay our respects to Victoria and the rest of the family."

As we headed up the interlocking brick walkway to the door, I counted eight vehicles packed into the long double-wide driveway. The last two barely fit and their back ends hung out slightly on the street. There were also a couple of cars alongside the curb in front of Harry's car. We climbed up three steps and stood on a small porch. Before Harry could raise his hand to knock, a tall, rather stern looking man opened the door. The scowly look on the man's face vanished as soon as he recognized Harry and it was instantly replaced with a smile. "Harry, my old friend. Come inside" His voice was loud and deep, as I somehow expected it to be. How is it that some voices suit their owners, while some sound as if they belong on an entirely different person? He stepped off to one side so we could enter the house. Then Harry and the man clasped hands in an earnest shake, before he pulled Harry into a hug and gave him a strong pat on the back.

"Lyle. So glad to see you, but so sorry for the circumstances that brought us together today. How are you holding up?" Harry asked.

Lyle shook his head up and down. "I'm doing okay. But my dear sister-in-law is not. Victoria is having a very hard time dealing with everything right now, which is understandable, of course."

"Yes, I'm sure Vic is devastated. It's quite a shock." Harry said.

"Oh, I'm sorry. I should have introduced you to my neighbor, Sydney." I think Harry suddenly realized he had forgotten I was there with him. He turned to me. "Sydney, this is Lyle, Bob's younger brother, and an old OPP colleague of mine. Lyle was in a different department than me, but we still ran into each other regularly."

"Lyle, please accept my deepest condolences." I managed to say. "I didn't know Bob well, as I only met him recently, when I joined the weekly bowling league where he worked. He was a super nice guy," I added. I felt as though I needed to justify my being there with Harry during this obviously personal time. I felt so uncomfortable in these situations. Death and funerals and crying were not my thing. I avoided them like the plague and would not have come today if it were not for Harry asking me to go with him "for support" he said, however I think he also wanted me there as a second set of eyes and ears. Harry remained convinced that something was wrong about Bob's death and that it wasn't an accident. He suggested I help him see what we could find out, hopefully while raising no suspicion.

"Thank you, Sydney. You're right, my brother was always so nice to people at work. He was a terrific guy." Lyle's deep voice was comforting, even with just a couple of words. Lyle turned his attention to Harry. "Come and see Victoria. You can put that tray of food on the counter with the others. Vic will be glad you are here, Harry." He led us to the kitchen where a gray-haired lady sat with two women trying to comfort her. "Victoria. Harry came to see you." The gray-haired woman looked up. She had red, swollen eyes from crying. She dabbed at the corners of her eyes with a wad of tissue.

"Oh, Harry." Victoria rose as Harry strode towards her. They embraced for a long hug as she sobbed into Harry's shoulder. Harry just held her and didn't say a word until they finally separated, and Victoria half fell back into her chair. I shuffled sideways and set the fruit tray on the long counter, where there were already about a dozen other trays of food sitting out.

"I am truly sorry, Vic. Bob was a great friend and husband, and this is just such a terrible loss." Harry pulled a chair close to Victoria's and held her shaking hand. They both just sat quietly, looking at each other for a moment. Neither spoke aloud nor moved. I stepped back and leaned against the kitchen wall. I shouldn't be here, I thought. This is for friends and family. I didn't belong here, and I wished myself invisible in that intimate exchange between two old friends who had lost a dear loved one. I looked around the room for a way to escape into the background, but Harry called me over.

"Sydney, come over here and meet Victoria Filmore. Bob's wife, and my old neighbor." I obeyed and stepped forward. "Victoria, this is my new neighbor, and friend, Sydney." I extended my hand in greeting, but Victoria stood quickly and pulled me into a tight squeeze.

"I'm a hugger." She explained. "Thank you for coming on this awful occasion. Harry needs a friend like you right now. Did you know Harry and Bob were so close?" Victoria asked, but continued before I could answer. "They used to go fishing together every chance they got. And if they weren't fishing, they were hanging out in Harry's garage, tinkering with something or other till all hours of the night." Victoria gushed about their friendship, giving me a better picture of what this loss meant for Harry. I hadn't realized they were so close.

All I could manage to say was, "I am very sorry for your loss." I found these types of situations most uncomfortable. I could feel my chest tighten, so I took a deep breath to ward off an anxiety attack. They really occurred at the most inopportune moments. The other two women who had been sitting with Victoria busied themselves in the kitchen, making coffee and unpacking the many trays of food people had brought over.

"Sit, please." Victoria patted the chair on the other side of her. So, I sat and listened to Harry and Victoria reminisce about past neighborhood BBQs, gatherings, card games, and some shenanigans that Bob and Harry had got up too. Finally, Harry brought up the "FOR SALE" sign on the front lawn, stating his surprise at the fact that he thought they would never sell their house. Victoria didn't seem too ready to talk about it and dismissed Harry's questions, stating they wanted to downsize, then quickly changed the subject. Glancing at my watch, I realized we had been visiting for the better part of two hours, and I had to work soon. Harry noticed and stood to give Victoria another big hug. "I am really so very sorry about Bob. I know you will miss him and so will I. I will drop by next week and we can chat more then. Please take care." Victoria sniffled and put on a brave smile as she nodded through her tears. By the time we got back outside, most of the cars in the driveway had gone, leaving only Victoria's car and Bob's brother Lyle's truck. Bob's giant boat of a car was probably still parked at the bowling alley, which gave me an idea.

"Hey Harry, I wonder if Bob left anything important in his old car. Maybe you could check it out while I'm at work this afternoon?"

"Good idea. I bet he stuffed his extra set of keys by his back plate."

Chapter 6

It was closing time at the bookshop, and I was getting ready to lock up when my phone rang. It was Matt. Or Detective Calhoon, I suppose, was more appropriate now. He wanted to talk to me about something and asked if I could meet him, so I waited for him out front of the shop. Not even five minutes later, Matt's police car pulled up. He rolled down the passenger window. "Hop in," he said.

I jumped in the front seat beside him. "You got here fast. Were you waiting around the corner or something?" I chuckled, but hoped not. That would be creepy.

"Pretty much." He laughed. "I wanted to make sure I caught you after you finished at Angela's." I picked up some coffee at Sally's. "I also brought one for you." He handed me one of Sally's large takeout cups. "Two cream, right? No sugar?"

"Uh ya. How did you know that?" Now I was getting concerned.

"Actually, I cheated. Sally told me what you usually order." Matt grinned. "Can we go for a drive and have a little chat? I need to ask you a few questions about the day you found Bob."

My stomach did a little flip. "Am I in trouble? Am I a suspect or something?"

"No, not at all Sydney. I am just trying to fill in a few of the blanks from that day." I breathed a sigh of relief.

"Well, in that case, sure. Since you brought me a coffee, how can I say no?" I chuckled. I also wanted to pick Matt's brain, but was doubtful he would volunteer much formal information about the investigation.

Matt wasted no more time getting to his questions. "Can you tell me about the day you found Bob's body? Starting with why you and Harry were there in the first place and that pickup truck you saw when you first arrived at Riverbowl? I know you already went through it with Detective Schroeder when he took your original statement, but I'm hoping you can remember a few more details." Matt pulled into a little park that overlooked the river. It was a beautiful spot. One that I had not previously discovered yet. There was a park bench set facing the river, and further down to the left, there was a dam with fast moving water, and a small historic building on the shore. Above the dam was a walkway that reached from one side of the river to the other. From our vantage point, we could look across the river and see part of Blueberry Falls downtown. I decided I would be returning here for one of my daily walks.

"Well," I started. "Harry mentioned I might pick up a few hours helping at the bar on weekends, as Riverbowl often got busy then. And he volunteered to take me because he wanted to talk to Bob, anyway. Harry said Bob had mentioned having something important to discuss with Harry, but he never had time to find out what it was about." I went over everything I could remember from that morning. The black pickup truck with the driver that I didn't get a proper look at. And I also brought up the Timmies coffee cup that was left on the ledge by lane four, where we found Bob's body. I told him I thought it was suspicious since there was also a warm coffee on Bob's desk already and a full pot still brewing. And Bob had made it clear he didn't allow anyone else back where all the machinery was because of the dangers. "So, why would there be a half full, still warm coffee back there if it didn't belong to someone else?" Matt took notes as I rambled on about every detail I could recall, rarely interrupting to ask questions, and instead, just letting me talk freely.

"How do you know it was warm and half full, Sydney?"

"Because I picked it up to check. Now, I think that was probably a bad idea. Touching things? But I wasn't thinking clearly, obviously."

"Hmmmm," was all that Matt said. He waited for me to continue.

I went through the last few details as best I could recall. "That's about it. Then you guys came in and asked us questions, then told us to leave. Can't think of anything else right now."

"That's good, Sydney. If you think of anything else, please call me." Matt handed me his detective business card.

"Matt, did you take that coffee cup in for evidence? Like for fingerprints or DNA or whatever you guys do?" I really hoped they had taken it for evidence. "Harry and I both thought it was strange it was back there."

"Yes, we did. Even though our original notion was that Bob's death was an accident."

"Original notion?" I asked. "Does that mean you are having second thoughts about the cause of death?"

"Well, that was the other thing I wanted to talk to you about. We couldn't get fingerprints off the cup, but we could get DNA from the lid." I didn't move or speak, as I wanted him to continue. Matt was sharing information with me! I stayed quiet and sipped my coffee, waiting for him to continue. "The lid did not match Bob's DNA. And nothing came up in the system to match it to. We need to find out who else was back there the day of Bob's death." Matt paused for a moment before continuing. "I think that truck you saw is important and I need to figure out who it belongs to."

Lifting my gaze from my cup, I stared at Matt. I'm sure my mouth dropped open like an idiot. "So, are you saying that Bob's death is not an accident?" My mind was racing now. Harry had been right. Something was off. "Who would want to hurt Bob? To kill Bob?!" I needed to talk to Harry right away about his friend. "He was right!"

"Who was right, Sydney?"

"Harry was! He said all along that something felt wrong and that he was not so sure Bob's death was an accident."

"Well, hang on Sydney." Matt interrupted. "I'm not saying that it wasn't an accident. What I am saying is that there was someone else on that platform with Bob on the day Bob died. They could have left, and then Bob fell. All we know for sure is that the DNA on the cup isn't Bob's. It's someone else's, and I need to find out who that person is."

I stared out the window of Matt's cruiser. My window was down slightly, and I could hear the roar of the water as it rushed through the dam. It was peaceful here. Ironic, I thought. Here we sat, in this peaceful place, enjoying a cup of Sally's delicious coffee, while discussing a potential murder that had occurred right around the corner.

Matt dropped me back off at Angela's Bookshop. I wanted to walk home from there because I had a couple of stops to make along the way. After he pulled away, I headed towards the hardware store. I needed to pick up some paint chips so I could finally get rid of the yucky green color in my bedroom. There were so many great selections, I ended up with a handful of color samples to take home. Next stop, I planned to pick up a beef pie at Sally's to heat up once I got home, but before I got there, I noticed Ellen and a young man I didn't recognize in the parking lot beside the hardware store. He appeared upset and was shouting something at her as she attempted to calm him down. I couldn't make out what either was saying. It didn't last long, and next thing, Ellen was giving the young man a hug and getting into her car as he walked over to a truck and they both drove off. I noted that the truck was black and similar to the one Harry and I had spotted at the bowling alley the day we found Bob. I would mention it to Harry tomorrow over our morning coffee.

Chapter 7

It was still dark outside when my phone buzzed. It was Harry who had messaged to tell me he had a pot of coffee on and already baked some cinnamon buns, which would be out of the oven shortly. His bribery technique to get me up and moving worked, and I quickly pulled on some sweatpants and a sweater, slipped on my runners, and headed out in the dark cool morning to cut across the lawn to Harry's house. It was convenient having a next-door neighbor like Harry. Since his retirement, he had taken to watching baking shows and trying new recipes. I was his taste tester. A job I did not mind at all, since I was an admitted sugar addict. Although I must admit that my recent new goal was to cut sugars out of my diet. So far, I was failing at this goal.

Harry handed me a coffee as soon as I walked through the door. "Thanks." I mumbled. I hugged the warm mug with my hands and took a sip as soon as I sat down. Wakefulness would come shortly for me. It appeared Harry had been up for quite a while already, and it was only 6:30am. He grabbed his own mug and sat down across from me. There was a plate of cinnamon buns on the table already. I reached for one. It was still warm and smelled delicious. "Are you okay? You look exhausted Harry." His eyes had dark circles underneath.

"I am," he admitted. "I tossed and turned all night, so I finally got up and decided I would start baking. At least it's something useful."

"Mmmm, it is useful." I managed between bites. "These are delicious! I'm sorry you didn't get much sleep, but I'm happy you baked this morning." Harry was a fantastic baker, and I appreciated being able to eat his goods as often as I did. "Hey Harry, did you have time to check out Bob's car yet?" I wiped the crumbs off my mouth.

"I did. But I found nothing out of the ordinary, so it wasn't helpful." Harry bit another chunk off his cinnamon bun and we both fell silent for a few minutes. Then Harry set his cup down on the table hard enough to make me jump. "Just can't get Bob's death off my mind." He blurted out. "I have seen many dead bodies in my day, and some are harder than others to deal with. But I just can't let go of this one, Syd. I still believe something was off when we found him, and I am not so sure it was an accident." Harry shook his head, repeating what he had expressed earlier when we first found Bob's body.

"Well, I think you might be right. And so does Matt." Harry stopped what he was doing.

"Why do you say that?"

"Matt told me yesterday after work. He had a few questions about the truck and wanted to go over what happened at the bowling alley the day we found Bob. Then, after I told him everything I could remember, I asked him about that coffee cup we saw on the ledge. He said they had got some DNA off it and it didn't match Bob or anyone else they could find in the system so far. So now, they are looking for suspects instead of writing it off as an accident."

"I knew it!" Harry jumped out of his chair and started pacing around the kitchen. "Everything felt wrong about the whole thing that day. The truck. Ellen in the washroom. The coffee cup. Bob's coffee still on his desk. And the back door left unlocked. Nothing adds up Syd." Harry sat back down and took a bite of his cinnamon bun. "And there's something else too that I wanted to tell you about that happened yesterday at Sally's over lunch." I waited impatiently for Harry to continue, but he sipped on his coffee and took another bite of bun before going further with his story. "I ran into George at the cafe and he had an interesting story to tell me. Do you remember George? You would likely have met him when you were bowling. He's the guy that gossips about everything and everyone. Half the time he's way off base, but the other half, he is bang on." I nodded yes.

"Yep. I remember him. Although I didn't get a chance to talk to him. He was the loud guy that sat at the other end of our table when we had wings and beer after bowling last week. What did he tell you?"

"Yep. That would be George. Loud and funny. But you gotta watch what you say, or it will be in the local paper the next day." Harry laughed. "So George comes over to my table and sits himself down and leans in as if he had something really important to say." My eyes were locked on Harry at this point. I just wanted him to get to the important stuff, but I waited quietly while he munched on more of his cinnamon bun. Good grief, Harry. Hurry up and tell me, would ya? My head screamed, but I kept my mouth shut. "George said that Ellen Caldwell and my friend Bob, my happily married friend, were having an affair for the last six months!" My eyes popped wide open.

"Noooo. Really?" I shook my head back and forth. "Well, that is an interesting bit of information, especially given the circumstances. Do you think Victoria knew about the affair? Do you think that's why they were selling their house?"

"I don't know what to think at this point, Syd. But I do know that Bob wanted to meet with me because he had something important to discuss. Except he never got the chance. Every bone in this old cop's body is telling me that Bob's death was no accident. And that I have to keep investigating it too. Matt Calhoon is a good detective, but he is up to his eyeballs with work right now. The police station is understaffed, and my old partner said they've seen a recent surge in local crimes, leaving everyone overworked. I don't want something to get missed in this investigation. So I am going to do whatever I can to figure out what happened to my friend. And I am going to need your help, Sydney. Will you help me?"

Before thinking through what Harry was really asking of me, I found the words, "of course I'll help you Harry," escaping from my mouth. Besides wanting to help my friend, my curious side desperately wanted to find out more now, too. So, I committed to helping Harry figure out how Bob Filmore had died last Monday. How did Bob's body end up behind the bowling pins, slumped over the pin setter machine, in lane four?

Chapter 8

I lay in my bed, staring at the walls and ceiling. Green. Like olives. I didn't like the color in my room. It probably hadn't been painted in at least a decade. The sample paint colors that I had picked up from the hardware store still sat on my dresser. I had been planning to paint since moving in, but still hadn't decided on a color yet. Maybe something bright and cheery? Like yellow. No. Not for my bedroom. That was more of a kitchen color. Paint color decisions would have to wait. After almost four months, I still didn't feel much of an urge to decorate or make the place my own. Hopefully, I would feel more settled soon.

My chest felt heavy again this morning. I hated that feeling. Like impending doom. Except nothing was happening right now, so I had no real reason to feel so anxious. But waking up here just didn't feel like home. I felt peaceful at home. At my old house. Not here yet. I liked my new house well enough but longed for my old home. My old life. That was gone now. I needed to make a new life now. Somehow. I got out of bed, threw my robe on and padded to the kitchen to make coffee. If I couldn't sleep, I might as well be up and doing something useful. My phone buzzed. Already? It was still early. It was Harry.

"Good. You're up." Harry didn't wait for my response. "I saw your lights on, so thought I'd see if you wanted to go for a brief road trip with me. I'll take you to Sally's first for breakfast."

"Where are we going after that?"

"I found out some interesting things about Ellen's ex-husband yesterday, so I want to go pay him a visit. Thought you would want to come too. He lives just outside of town, so not far. I'll update you over breakfast. Can you be ready in a half hour?" Harry was chomping at the bit, and I guessed he had already been up for a while, likely watching for my kitchen lights, knowing him.

"Can you give me an hour Harry? I want to have a shower and I have a couple of things to do first, then I'm free?"

"Sure. Meet you outside in an hour. I'll drive."

After showering, I quickly called Natalie. Yesterday, I promised her I'd call this morning for a chat. I told her about the bake-off that Angela had roped me into and asked her which recipe she thought would be best. "I can't think of one right now, Syd, but why don't you look through your grandma's old recipe book? You used to bake from that all the time, and everything was delicious. I'm sure you'll find a winner in there."

"That's a great idea, Nat! I am heading out this morning with Harry on a little road trip, but I will definitely do that afterwards." Changing focus, I inquired about things in my old neighborhood. "How are things there? Have you seen Gerard lately?"

"He was over visiting Greg a couple of days ago, but I stayed inside. He didn't stay long because his new girlfriend was sitting in the car waiting for him."

"Oh," was all I managed. "I have to run now. Harry will be waiting for me. Talk to you later." I hung up and ran out the door.

***

I slid into the passenger seat of Harry's new Explorer. Unlike the mess of my car, Harry's vehicle was spotless, and it still had that new car smell. We didn't talk on the three-minute trip to Sally's Café. I was awake but hungry and not feeling overly chatty yet. Unable to find a parking spot on the road in front of the cafe, Harry drove to the town lot across the street instead. On some mornings, the cafe was so full that customers had to wait for a table. We got lucky today and found one stuffed in a back corner. Sally's breakfasts were delicious, and it was her busiest time of day. We drank our coffees while we waited for our orders.

"So, what did you find out yesterday?" I was curious to hear what Harry had learned.

Harry leaned in to avoid being overheard. "After learning about the possibility of Ellen and Bob having a secret affair, I had a chat with my old partner, Mark, to see what he could dig up. I'm still having a hard time wrapping my head around Bob stepping out on Victoria, and I'm still not sure if it's true, but we have to start somewhere."

Sally stopped by to see if we needed a top up on our coffees while we waited. "Might be a bit, guys. The place is packed, and my cook arrived late this morning. Sally was a big, jolly looking lady that I guessed to be in her mid sixties. She was full of energy and smiles and baked the best coconut cream pie I had ever tasted. She served a big hearty breakfast seven days a week and never skimped on portions. I hadn't found another cafe anywhere nearby that could match her food or service. No wonder the place was always packed.

"No rush, my dear." Harry put his hand on Sally's. "We're just happy to have got a table this morning. You are jam packed today." Harry and Sally had been friends since childhood. They went to the same schools growing up, and I believe they may have even dated for a while, once upon a time. I really needed to find out more about that one day. Sally left and Harry went back to updating me.

As soon as Sally was out of earshot, Harry started filling me in about what he had learned from his old partner. “Ellen Caldwell has a powerful motive if there is any truth in the rumor about her affair with Bob. And she was at Riverbowl already when we found Bob’s body. But her record is clean. Not so much as a speeding ticket in the last ten years. However, it turns out that Ellen’s ex-husband Eddie spent a bit of time in jail for getting into a drunken bar fight a couple of years back. The fight wouldn’t have been so bad, but I guess Eddie has a temper, and he laid a beating on some guy from out of town. The guy ended up in hospital with a broken nose and a couple of cracked ribs.” My eyebrows raised. Apparently, the fight was over Ellen. They were married at the time, but Ellen left him because of Eddie’s drinking. They have a son who is around twenty years old now.”

“Oh wow. That is interesting. Wonder if Eddie knew about Bob and Ellen’s affair?”

“Possibly. I wondered the same thing. So, I went to see his parole officer yesterday. Eddie did his time in jail and says he’s been sober ever since. Says he’s trying to turn his life around. His parole officer backs him up on that. He is living out at his Uncle Gus’ farm and took over his small engine repair business. Gus retired this year and took off south to Florida with his new lady. I figure we should go pay Eddie a visit today and see what he's been up to. It's about fifteen minutes north of town."

We headed out the north end of town and turned onto a side road that I hadn't explored yet. During the first month living in Blueberry Falls, I had spent a lot of my days off just driving around exploring many back roads and various locations to help situate myself and get a handle on my unfamiliar surroundings. I felt like a fish out of water still in many ways here. My old city life was nothing like Blueberry Falls. So far, I had learned that the area had small pockets of cleared farmland, but the land here was rugged, and not the best for farming. Dense bush, rocky terrain, and many hills and valleys covered much of the region. The region was called The Highlands, and Blueberry Falls was only one of many small towns within. There were also some interesting little hamlets which I thought were in the oddest, off the traveled path locations. Remnants of some of the original settlements from the old pioneers. A railway line, originally North and Pacific Junction Railway, I believe, ran through Blueberry Falls, linking towns in south Muskoka to North Bay. As far as I knew, the train ran regularly, and passed through Blueberry Falls at least three times each day. As the train approached roads and intersections, the conductor would blast the train whistle repeatedly, warning all in its path. I could clearly hear the horn from my house, and it carried for quite a distance. At first, I was aware of it every time it blasted, but as time went on, I got used to it, and many times, didn't notice it at all anymore.

As Harry drove, we planned what we would do once we got to Eddie's place. With Eddie's history of a bad temper, Harry warned me to keep the questions light and not accusatory. After traveling along a winding dirt road for about 15 minutes, we turned onto a smaller sideroad and went another kilometer before eventually stopping at a long narrow graveled laneway. "That's Gus Caldwell's place down there." Harry pointed towards an old two-story farmhouse that sat at the end of the laneway. As we drove slowly down the lane, I took in the scenery. Cedar rail fencing flanked the driveway on both sides, then continued across the property's roadside in opposite directions, farther than I could see. Both sides had big shelters, and each housed a couple of horses. It was beautiful. I would love to live in a place like this one day, although that was doubtful, considering my financial circumstances now. Divorce had forced me to adjust my lifestyle, and I was still getting used to it. Although the farmhouse looked old, it looked as if it had recently received a fresh coat of blue paint. There was a freshly painted white covered porch that wrapped around from the front and all the way down the west side of the house. There were large perennial gardens that ran from the porch to the well manicured front lawn.

The gardens were overflowing with flowers of all kinds, most of which I recognized, but could not name. Some plants, like the roses, were still in full bloom, which surprised me since it was already approaching late September. Everything looked well kept, and the gardens accented the house beautifully. I wondered who did all the gardening.

Harry parked his car in front of the house. "That's Eddie's truck, so I'm guessing he's around here somewhere." Harry pointed at a big black Dodge truck parked beside a giant red tractor. "Let's go find him and have a chat." In that moment, I could imagine Harry as a cop back in the day. His stance had changed somewhat as soon as we started walking towards the house. Taller somehow. Bigger, somehow. I followed along behind him, planning to leave all the talking to him. After all, Harry was an old pro at this kind of thing, and I was just an amateur sleuth with an overly inquisitive mind that got roped into helping Harry find Bob's killer.

Before we got to the porch stairs, the front door swung open and a tall, wiry man with dark curly hair sticking out from under a Toronto Blue Jay's cap stepped out onto the porch and stood at the top of the stairs, basically blocking our path. Harry and I stopped at the bottom step, looking up. "Hey, Eddie. How have you been?" Harry had dropped his authoritative tone of minutes early and took on a more casual voice and stance. He stretched out his arm in greeting, waiting for Eddie to shake his hand.

"What do you want, Harry? Don't tell me this is just a friendly visit between a couple of old friends. You know we were never friends." Harry dropped his extended hand. Formal and friendly greetings were out of the question right now, apparently. Harry changed to a more direct approach.

"We just want to ask you a couple of questions. About Bob. This is my neighbor, Sydney." Harry nodded in my direction.

"Hi." I said. Eddie didn't acknowledge me at all. He stepped to the edge of the top step and put a hand on each rail, leaning forward slightly. His whole body stiffened, and he drew his mouth into a tight, straight line, as if trying to stop any words from escaping. I noticed he had a scar that ran along the top of his left cheekbone. The faded scar was barely visible and didn't look fresh. He had the beginnings of a salt and pepper beard. He wore brown coveralls and a plaid flannel shirt, both scattered with dirt and oil stains. In all his ruggedness, he had the most piercing blue eyes I had ever seen, and it was easy to imagine the good-looking young man he likely once was.

"I thought you retired from the force, Harry."

"Oh, I did. This isn't an official visit of any kind. I just wanted to ask you a few questions. Bob was my friend, and I just need to satisfy my curiosity about Bob's accident." Using the word "accident" was apparently an excellent tactic because Eddie relaxed his stance a bit. But instead of inviting us up onto his porch, he walked down the stairs, forcing us to step aside, then walked right past us toward the barn.

"Okay. You can ask. But I got things to do, so you're gonna have to follow me out here and talk while I work. Old Hank Manning is coming out later today to pick up his chainsaw and I haven't got it fixed yet." The barn was surprisingly organized and tidy. There were two long work benches. Chainsaws, presumably awaiting Eddie's repair or servicing, covered one workbench. The other bench was mainly clear except for a single chainsaw, with pieces lined up neatly. Eddie started putting the saw back together with ease. This was obviously something he had done often. I glanced around the barn. Above the bench was a large sign mounted on the wall with faded lettering. "The Caldwell Bros. Small Engine Repairs. Call Gus or Archie" and then a phone number, so faded, I couldn't quite make out all the numbers. Eddie noticed me looking at the sign. "This used to be my dad and Uncle Gus' shop, but I took over after dad died, and Uncle Gus retired." I was surprised by Eddie's offer of insight.

"Oh, cool." I said stupidly. Sometimes, I really was socially awkward. Ugh.

"What do you wanna ask me, Harry? Might as well get right to it so you two can be on your way, and I can get my work done. I haven't been doing anything since getting out 'cept working here mostly and spending time with my boy, so I don't know why you are here."

Harry got straight to the point. "I heard the other day that your ex-wife might have been having a secret fling." Eddie set the chainsaw down on the bench and turned around. Harry looked directly at him. "Do you know anything about that, Eddie?"

"What does that have to do with Bob? I thought you said you wanted to ask questions about Bob's accident. This doesn't sound like that." Eddie had once again gained his stiffened stance. "I changed my mind about answering questions about Bob's accident. I've got too much work to do and don't have time for chats. So, you guys can both leave now." And with that said, Eddie turned his back to us and started working on the chainsaw with a fury. He didn't give us another glance.

"Okay, we'll go now." Harry and I exited the barn and drove home in silence. The visit was not as fruitful as we had hoped, as we couldn't very well force Eddie to talk to us. As Harry drove, I checked my messages. Angela had left one earlier asking if I could work for a couple hours after lunch, saying she had a last-minute appointment pop up. When I got home, I messaged her back and told her I could be there in an hour. As I looked in the hall mirror, I quickly ran a comb through my hair and considered if I needed to change my clothes before work. I was hungry and wanted to grab a bite to eat before work, and that took precedence over clothing attire right then. I grabbed my wallet and keys and rushed back out the door to go to Sally's Cafe for some takeout.

Chapter 9

I needed to talk to Ellen and ask her some questions. I wanted to sort out fact from fiction, so I decided to drop in on my way home from work. Our visit to Ellen's ex-husband Eddie had not been fruitful. Hopefully, Ellen's would go better, I thought as I drove the short distance from Angela's Bookshop to Ellen's house. I turned into Ellen Caldwell's driveway and parked behind her car. There was an older black Dodge pickup truck parked beside her car. I pulled out my phone and took a few pictures of the truck because it looked a lot like the one I had seen the other day at Riverbowl. But then again, half the town owned pickup trucks, and many were black or dark colored. Something I hadn't noticed until that day at Riverbowl. Now, everywhere I turned, there was another pickup. As I stepped out of my car, I saw a truck parked across the road from Ellen's driveway pull out quickly and drive away. It was also black. Seriously? Does every single person in Blueberry Falls own a black truck? Because it sure seemed that way. I shook my head and headed up the driveway to talk to Ellen. As I approached her door, I realized I should have called ahead, instead of just showing up on her doorstep, but it was a spur-of-the-moment decision to stop in on my way home from work.

I knocked on the door and instant warning yaps sounded, coming from some kind of smaller dog, by the high-pitched noises I was hearing. "Just a minute!" I heard Ellen calling. "Stella, quiet. Go lay down." The yapping came to an immediate halt. Ellen partially opened the door, her leg blocking access to a small dog that was trying desperately to get to me. "Stella, go lay down. Right now." Ellen's assertiveness was a change from her usual quietness that I had experienced so far. Stella turned and headed off somewhere, so Ellen opened the door more for me. "Sydney. This is a surprise. What are you doing here?"

"I'm sorry I didn't call first. I was just on my way home from work and wanted to stop in and see how you were doing. I haven't seen you since ….. well, since we found Bob." I lowered my eyes, now fully aware that my boldness was probably rude, seeing as I didn't know Ellen all that well. "You were so upset that day I wanted to check up on you. It's not every day that one finds a body, never mind, one of a friend. It must have been quite a shock for you." At the mention of Bob's name, Ellen's eyes immediately glistened with the beginnings of tears, and I thought she might begin crying right there on her doorstep. But she quickly pulled herself together and stepped back to let me inside. "Do you want to come in and have a coffee? Or tea, if you'd rather? I've got both.

"Yes, thanks. I'd love a coffee. It was a busy last couple hours at work and I didn't get a chance for a break at all." I stepped into her entranceway. To the right was the kitchen, and straight ahead was a lovely, sunken living room. The dog must have decided I wasn't all that interesting and was curled up on a fluffy dog bed that was set between the edge of a large L-shaped couch and a leather recliner, apparently already asleep. "I didn't know you had a truck." I tried to sound casual, but my casual always came out so stilted.

"Oh, that's Nathan's truck. My son. He is nearly twenty and lives in the basement. He's been trying to save up for a place of his own, but everything is so expensive these days." As if on cue, a door opened, presumably leading to the basement, and a tall young man stepped into the kitchen. The same tall young man I had seen arguing with Ellen by the hardware store the other day.

"I'm heading out now, Mom."

"Oh Nate. This is Sydney. She's new in town and has just joined our bowling league. Sydney, this is my son, Nate."

"Nice to meet you, Nate." We shook hands briefly, but he wouldn't meet my eyes.

"Hi," was all he said back. "See you later, Mom," He said as he walked out the door.

I sat at the kitchen table while Ellen put on a pot of coffee. It had become quite a habit for me lately, sitting in other people's kitchens waiting for them to make me coffee. Not a bad habit at all, I thought. I looked around the room while I waited. In the corner, there was a door leading to the backyard. Beside that, on a counter, sat a vase full of flowers that looked like they were reaching the end of their days, and I wondered if they had come from her secret affair; if what George had told us was, in fact, true. I needed to ask her about it because I didn't want to rely solely on George's gossip channel. His unreliability was well known; he frequently repeated hearsay with no regard for accuracy. I guess that was what gossip was, anyway. Mostly, untruth and embellishments from bored people, unhappy with their own lives.

Victoria hadn't even hinted at trouble in the marriage when we were there, and although Harry was still curious about the important news that Bob had wanted to talk to him about, he had never mentioned his marriage being in trouble. Even Eddie's angry reaction, when Harry mentioned the affair, wasn't proof of any truth in it either. Bob and Victoria's house was for sale, though. And Bob had never mentioned that to Harry. Plus, Victoria had definitely been reluctant to talk about it when Harry mentioned the new "For Sale" sign on the front lawn. Then again, only one day after her husband's death, Victoria was likely feeling extremely lost and overwhelmed with grief. I could only imagine what that was like. Personally, I hadn't lost many people that I was really close to so far in my life. Losing my elderly grandparents was probably the most significant because we were so close. And I suppose I had also lost my husband, but that was just the death of a marriage, instead of the death of a person, so it wasn't the same. Although, I believe I was still grieving over my lost marriage, if I was being truthful with myself. Food for thought for a later day. I shoved it aside and looked up at Ellen as she set a big steamy mug of coffee down in front of me, along with a plateful of peanut butter cookies. Oh boy, I was going to have to kick up my exercise routine with all the sweets I'd been having lately.

"Thanks." I quickly reached for a cookie. "Peanut butter. One of my favs." I mumbled between bites. I glanced again toward the flowers. Ellen followed my gaze. "Those look nice. Secret admirer?" As soon as the words were out of my mouth, I wished I had reworded my question to be more tactful. Once again, Ellen's eyes filled with tears, and she rose from the table to busy herself at the counter with her back to me. "I'm so sorry. I didn't mean to upset you. They are lovely flowers." The emotional responses must have had to do with finding Bob's body. I didn't know how long they had been friends, but if I had ever found Natalie's body, I would be extremely upset. Or maybe the rumors were true and Ellen was having an affair with Bob. That would explain her crying at every other word.

Ellen turned and set another plate of goodies beside the still full plate of peanut butter cookies. "That's okay Sydney. I guess I'm just still emotional after seeing Bob laying so lifeless like that. I've never seen anything like it. Certainly, I've witnessed some upsetting sights at the animal shelter, but Bob was a true friend." Tears ran down her cheeks as she sipped her coffee and quietly sniffed. She dabbed her nose with a tissue and wiped her eyes with the back of her hands. Ellen was a quiet spoken, gentle spirited person, from what I could tell so far. She even volunteered at the local animal shelter a couple of hours a week. She had a soft spot for strays and unwanted animals, is what she told me the other week when I had driven her home from the alley.

"I need to ask you something personal and I don't want to upset you more, but I have to know if what I heard was true or simply rumors." Ellen tilted her head. So I took it as a sign to keep going. "Were you and Bob having an affair?" I blurted out.

Ellen's head shot up and she stared directly at me. Her mouth had tightened into a straight line. "What? Why would you ask me that? Who said that?" Her immediate reaction had me second guessing my decision to verify George's rumor, but I needed to know.

I continued pushing. "Is it true?" My query was as gentle as possible. As a guest in her kitchen, I was well aware that I was crossing boundaries. I chose to keep my source undisclosed. "I heard talk at Sally's Cafe the other day, and after hearing you and Bob arguing, then when I asked about the flowers, in fact, your emotional reaction every time I say Bob's name, I thought maybe there was some truth in it." I studied her closely. "Is that where the flowers came from? Are they from Bob? I am sorry to upset you, but this is important." Oh crap, I immediately wished I hadn't stressed the importance of this truth, as Matt had instructed me not to share any information about the fact that Bob's death may not, in fact, be accidental. Well, the floodgates opened right up. Ellen sobbed loudly. Loud enough for her dog to come running into the kitchen and start jumping up on her leg. She bent and scooped the dog up into her lap and hugged her in her arms, burying her face into the long fur. "You loved him, didn't you?" Ellen didn't need to speak for me to get verification of the affair. After a few minutes, she set the dog down on the floor and pulled herself together enough to talk to me.

"Yes, I loved Bob. And yes, we had an affair, which, by the way, I am not proud of at all. I never imagined myself as a woman who would interfere with a relationship by getting involved with a married man. I am now that woman. A home wrecker. And apparently, the whole town knows it." She blew her nose and sipped her coffee. She wouldn't look at me as she continued. "We had an affair for almost a year. But when it began, Bob told me he was separated and in the midst of a divorce. I believed him until I found out otherwise. By then, I was already in love with him and couldn't bear to lose him. I wish it had never happened, but it did, and I can't take it back. The night you heard us argue, I gave Bob an ultimatum because he had been promising me for so long that he was going to tell his wife everything and leave her. He never did. That night at the bowling alley, Bob had told me he wanted to end our affair. He said he was ending it with me and wanted to fix things with his wife. He chose Victoria. He didn't want me. Said he still loved her and wanted to fix everything. He broke my heart. I told him I hated him. And now he's dead. Those were the last words I ever said to him."

"Did Bob send you those flowers?"

"Yes. Well, I thought so. But that night, when I asked him why he would send flowers if he was planning to break up with me, he denied it. Said he never sent them. Said he didn't know what I was talking about. And I didn't believe him. I told him he shouldn't have played with my heart like that. I got mad. Real mad. After I told Bob I hated him, I stormed out of his office and ran into the washroom. When I got myself calmed down, I was heading back to have a drink with all you guys and drink my anger and sadness away. That's when I ran into you."

"So, if those flowers aren't from Bob, then who are they from?"

"That's the thing. I have no idea. And honestly, sending flowers wasn't something Bob would usually do. But I have no idea who sent them if it wasn't him. And I accused Bob of being a liar and called him one that night.!" Ellen burst into tears again. "Gosh, Sydney, you must think I am an absolutely horrible person." Actually, I was not a fan of home wreckers for sure, especially since my husband just threw away our marriage because of a stupid home wrecker, but truth be told, I blamed my husband far more than that other woman. After all, he was the one that took the vows with me. Not her.

I still had more questions for Ellen. "Why were you at the bowling alley on Monday morning when we found Bob?" It seemed strange to me that Ellen would look for him if she had told him she hated him and he had ended the relationship.

"Bob had sent me a message that morning, asking me if I would meet him at the alley. He said he had a couple of my things still and wanted to return them. He apologized for how things ended on Thursday night. I was secretly hoping he had changed his mind and wanted to be with me. But when I got there, I couldn't find him. That's when I ran into you and that's when we found, when we….." Ellen broke down, and I decided not to push things any further. I consoled her for a little while longer, finished my coffee and left, with promises to check in on her again soon.

Chapter 10

It was Monday, and I had the day off, so my plan was to figure out what the heck I was going to bake for Saturday's bake-off at the Blueberry Falls annual fall fair. I had promised Angela that I would do my best in representing Angela's Bookshop because she couldn't be there this year to compete, but I was doubtful my best would win any ribbons against the other fantastic bakers that entered every year. I had to at least try. However, I couldn't even decide what I would bake yet. I flipped through my grandma's old worn recipe book. My treasure. Surely there was something in here that I knew how to bake well that was worthy of a small-town bake-off between Main Street businesses. My grandma had gifted me this treasure trove of her favorite recipes many years ago, just before she passed, when I was a young teenager. Thinking about grandma now still made my heart hurt in my chest. I felt the loss of my grandparents, both in their late eighties, for a long time after their deaths, even though they had lived good lives.

Seeing each recipe as I turned the pages brought back some wonderful memories of Sunday afternoons spent with my grandma. She had inspired my love for baking. We would spend many hours in her kitchen, baking pies and cakes and so many types of cookies I couldn't even remember half of them. Grandma would let me eat all the cookies that broke when she set them on the cooling trays. This is where I think I found my love for sugary treats. It's a wonder I wasn't three hundred pounds. There was a large cookstove in their farmhouse where she would bake bread all winter long. Their home was so cozy, and I just loved visiting. Grandpa spent much of his time outside on the tractor or with their livestock in the magnificent, massive, century old barn. They had a herd of cattle and at least four or five horses most times. They finally had to sell all their livestock when Grandpa could no longer manage all the chores necessary to take care of them. And since we lived about an hour away, my parents weren't able to come help often enough. I turned the page of the cookbook, and suddenly I knew exactly what I would bake. Of course! Grandma's version of a French Apple Cake! This was one of her favorites. And mine too. She would usually bake it for the fall fairs in the little town where my grandparents lived, and she usually came home with a red ribbon. If I could pull this off, I might even earn a prize. I now had a little more hope since there were only five or six entries in total. The judges handed out ribbons to the top three contestants. It's funny how much a little ribbon can mean. It reminded me of when we had the cross-country runs at school. Everyone was so excited to win those little red and blue ribbons. I quickly skimmed through the recipe to remind myself how to make the cake. I used to know it from memory, but that was a long time ago. There were quite a few steps involved and hopefully, I could perfect the cake for Saturday. Contestants could not use written recipes during the bake-off. So, with nothing to refer to, I would have to commit it to memory before the contest began. It had been a while since I last baked it, so it might take me a few practice runs. I wanted to spend the morning baking while I had time. I would take the finished cake over to Harry. He would surely appreciate that, I think. He also had quite a sweet tooth. I scanned the ingredients list, then checked my cupboard. Oh shoot. I didn't even have half the needed ingredients. I had baked nothing since moving here from Barrie. In fact, I barely even cooked my dinner lately. I closed the cupboard door, took a photo of the recipe with my phone and headed out the door to go to the grocery store. Although this would delay my baking plan slightly, I could be back home within the hour and still have the rest of the day to bake.

As soon as I got outside, the chill air hit me. It was late September, so I guess that was to be expected. I zipped up my jacket and started down my driveway to my car. "What the heck! Are you kidding me?" I said out loud to the crisp fall air. My front driver's side car tire was flat. Not just a little flat. Completely flat. So weird. I didn't notice a problem last night when I parked it. No warnings had alerted me to low air. As I bent down to examine the tire, I noticed a hole right through the side of it. It looked like someone had purposely done this. But why? And by who? I looked around, but there was no one in sight. A shiver ran down my spine. I would have to call someone to come because it was obvious the tire was beyond repair and changing tires was not my forte. Another expense I really couldn't afford right now, but there was nothing I could do about it. I needed my car. Small town living meant no bus service, and walking was out of the question for most destinations. I would ask Harry who to call. He would know. And maybe he could also take me for a quick trip to the grocery store so I could at least still do my baking today. As I stood up, I saw a folded piece of paper on my front windshield, tucked under the wiper blade. I looked around but couldn't see anyone at all. I pulled the paper out from under the wiper and unfolded it. My stomach lurched, and I quickly whipped my head in all directions. Still saw no one. The note had a message written in bold capital letters. Presumably to me. "MIND YOUR OWN BUSINESS IF YOU KNOW WHAT'S GOOD FOR YOU." I pocketed the note, took some photos of the ruined tire, and quickly stomped off to Harry's house.

I banged loudly on Harry's door. I was well aware that he wasn't expecting me this morning and his hearing seemed to be a bit lacking at times. I was steaming mad and didn't have the patience to wait, so I banged again. "What is all the banging about?" Harry asked me as he pulled the door open. "Give an old man time to get up from his recliner, would ya?" Harry stepped back to let me in. "What has got you all rattled this morning, girl?"

I stepped inside and shoved the note towards Harry. "This!" Harry took the note and carefully unfolded it to read. "Someone slashed my tire, too! Who would do this, Harry?" My strong composure crumbled, and I slumped into one of Harry's kitchen chairs, while fumbling for my phone to show him the photo of my ruined tire. When I showed him the picture, Harry said nothing. He sat down and pulled a chair right in front of mine, while shaking his head back and forth.

"I'm afraid this is probably my fault for dragging you into this investigation with me, Sydney. I'm so sorry. I have obviously put you in danger and I should never have asked you to help me find out what happened to Bob." Harry handed the note back to me and sat back in his chair. "We need to go down to the police station and make a report right away. We should also call Matt and tell him about it. He needs to see this." Harry waved the note. "He will have to assign someone to keep an eye on you, I think. To keep you safe."

"What?! No way Harry! I'm not having some cop following me and watching my every move! That's ridiculous!" My defeated feelings quickly turned into anger. "And this is definitely not your fault, either. I told you I would help you because I wanted to. If someone wants to scare me, that's not your fault. I don't know who left me this note and slashed my tire, but I am sure we have struck a nerve and someone is nervous about our investigation of Bob's death. And I will bet you it's Eddie! He was mad when we brought up his ex-wife's affair with Bob. And you said he had a bad temper and a drinking problem. Someone like that could definitely be guilty of slashing my tire. Plus, didn't you say Eddie had spent time in jail?"

Harry sat quietly, waiting for me to calm down before saying anything. "Okay, how about this? We keep a quieter profile while investigating. Plus, we get a couple of cameras set up outside your house so we can keep a better eye on you. And we get you set up with a security alarm. I will feel a whole lot better if you will agree to that." I nodded my head up and down at Harry in agreement. He continued. "And about Eddie. You might be right, but we shouldn't jump to any conclusions. Just because Eddie spent time in jail doesn't mean he had anything to do with Bob's death. And flying off the handle because his ex-wife might have been having an affair might be nothing more than Eddie getting defensive over Ellen. It's not evidence of anything." Harry paused, letting what he said sink in. "I will drive you over to the police station so you can file that report, and then we can go see about getting someone out to put a new tire on your car. Later, we can go through our next steps on how we will proceed with investigating my friend's death. Sound good?" Harry always had to be so damned logical, but it helped a lot.

"Yep. Sounds good. Oh, and Harry, would you mind taking me to the grocery store too?" I explained about my commitment to Angela for the bake-off, and my need to finalize my recipe choice before the end of the day, so I could submit it to the committee or whoever handled the organizing of the contest.

Chapter 11

Well, my day started on a low note with the tire incident, but it hadn't been a total wash. After Harry took me for baking ingredients (which he happily did after I promised him he could be my taste tester), I successfully baked the French Apple Cake I planned to share with Harry once I was all done. I spent the next hour cleaning up my baking mess and writing out the list of ingredients I needed to submit to Mrs. Maple, the lady in charge of organizing the bake-off. Contestants had to submit their ingredient list by Wednesday afternoon, so we would be sure to have the items available. I wanted to send them to her today, to be sure I didn't forget. Once done, I head across my lawn, dessert in hand, feeling proud as a peacock.

The cake turned out perfect and Harry insisted it would be the winner at any bake-off. I had even made an apple strudel with the extra apples I had bought. I put the strudel in the fridge for a later snack or future bribery needs. Baking again felt good, and I was pleased to finally christen my kitchen with some proper use instead of the throw together meals I had been cooking so far. Since I was in the spirit, I took a roast out of the freezer so I could cook it up tomorrow. I would invite Harry to come for dinner. I had been a regular and frequent visitor in his kitchen since moving here, and it was about time I repaid him, a bit at least. We both indulged in testing hearty servings, which was then washed down with a big glass of milk, leaving us feeling far too full to do too much energetic wise. By the time I returned to my house, I felt ready for a nap. I would blame it on a sugar crash. I was just dozing off when my phone rang. Crap.

"Hello." I said rather gruffly. I didn't recognize the number. This better be important, I thought.

"Ummm, Sydney?" The voice on the other end was familiar, but I didn't recognize it right away. I sat up and tried to wake myself properly. I just hate it when I am torn out of a nap abruptly. Initially, I'm always disoriented for the first few seconds.

"Yep. You got me."

"It's Ellen. Am I calling at a bad time?" Well yes, actually, you are.

"No, not at all. Sorry. Was just in the middle of something. What's up?" Yes, I was just in the middle of a well-deserved nap.

"You said it would be all right if I called you...... If I wanted to chat. So, I thought I would see if you wanted to go for a coffee with me, over at Sally's?"

"Sure. I'd love to. I could use a coffee. Can you give me half an hour?" When I looked down at my shirt, I noticed flour splatters across the front of it. I hadn't bothered to change it for my visit with Harry, but that's not a public coffee shop. I glanced at my watch. It was almost 4. "Say, 4:30? Would that work?"

"Yes, perfect. See you then." Ellen hung up, and I got up and headed to the bathroom to splash some water on my face, then went about the business of cleaning myself up enough to be presentable at Sally's. Which wasn't much, really. I threw on a fresh shirt, grabbed my jacket, and headed out. I decided I would walk, as I figured it might help wake me up properly, and shake off my tired, draggy feeling. The walk was short. Less than ten minutes. As I rounded the last corner onto Main Street, I could see the brightly colored "Sally's Café" sign, sporting a picture of a giant steaming mug. It was only a few buildings down from the corner.

I spotted Ellen's red car as she pulled into an empty spot across the street from the cafe. A man with a funky jacket and wild hair quickly approached her as she was crossing the road, stopping her. I recognized him, and the jacket, but couldn't remember where from. He held a bouquet. By this time, I had already reached Sally's. I waved but Ellen didn't notice, so I just stood outside the cafe waiting for Ellen and curiously watching the interaction. It appeared strange, and Ellen looked uncomfortable, as she shifted from foot to foot, while looking down at the ground. The man was holding out the flowers for Ellen, I assumed, but when her arms didn't reach out to take them, he practically stuffed them into her hands. She hesitated before taking hold of them. Strange. The man was saying something to her, but from where I stood, I couldn't hear anything but the noise of passing cars, which also kept blocking my view. As the man spoke, Ellen shook her head back and forth, in what looked to me like a solid no. She held the flowers out as if trying to return them to the man. Clearly, she was uncomfortable, so I decided it was time to intervene.

"Ellen!" I called loud, so she could hear me. "Ellen!" I tried again. She looked up, and I waved as I began to cross the street. The man turned quickly and was gone before I got across the street. She opened her car door, and carelessly tossed the flowers on the front seat, then slammed it shut and walked towards me, before I got all the way across. I turned and went back to the other side with Ellen.

"Oh good. Glad you're here already. Let's go get that coffee, shall we?" Ellen smiled, but the look of concern that washed across her face did not match the smile she had pasted on.

"Who was that man? I recognized him from somewhere but couldn't quite place him."

"Oh, that was Marty. You met him already at bowling. He was Harry's last-minute replacement." Sally's wasn't busy, and I was happy that we got my favorite table in the corner by the window.

"Yes, of course! That's where I've seen him before. Not sure how I could have forgotten that jacket of his." I laughed.

"Right?!" Ellen was already looking more relaxed.

"Flowers. Hmmm. I didn't know you and him were a thing?"

"Oh my God, no Sydney! We most definitely are NOT. And I've told him as much. But he just doesn't seem to get the message." Ellen quieted her voice back to her normal volume. "He asked me to dinner just now, when he gave me the flowers. I told him no. Again! He already asked me a few days ago. I said no then too, but maybe I didn't make it clear enough that I am not interested in going to dinner with him, or anywhere else. Ever. Today I said as much. I even tried to give the flowers back, but he refused to take them. I didn't want to throw them on the ground right there. Maybe I'll just give them away to someone. Do you want them?"

"No, thanks though." I snickered and rolled my eyes. She laughed.

"I'm so glad you interrupted him when you did. It got rid of him. At least for now. He makes me feel so uncomfortable. He is awfully creepy, don't you think?"

"I don't know him. I've never said more than a few words to him that night at bowling when he wanted to drive you home, but you went with me instead. But yes, I think he's got a weird vibe. Maybe he's just an awkward guy with a crush, trying to fit in." I mused.

"Maybe so, but I wish he would just leave me alone. I've got enough to worry about."

"Next time he bugs you, call me and I am happy to come over and rescue you again. If there is a next time. Hopefully, he got the message today."

"Thanks, I'll do that."

I leaned forward and put my hand across the table onto Ellen's. "Was there something specific you wanted to talk to me about today?"

"Nothing important. Just wanted to get out and see a friendly face. Get to know you more."

"How are you holding up, anyway?"

Ellen shook her head slowly. "Oh, you know. Up and down. But I am doing okay, I guess."

A thought suddenly came to mind. "You don't think those other flowers that you got were from Marty, do you? I mean, didn't you say that Bob flat out denied sending them? Which would be weird if he sent them."

"I bet you're right! I never even thought of Marty." We both sat quietly and sipped on our coffees, deep in thoughts of our own.

Chapter 12

I took a deep breath before opening the door to the Blueberry Falls police station. Although I had been here just yesterday with Harry to file the report about my slashed tire, today made me nervous. Matt had called me first thing this morning and asked me to "come down to the station for a chat" was how he put it. He sounded very official over the phone and it didn't feel to me that this was going to be a friendly chat, by the tone of his voice and his curtness during the call. He stated it was concerning the threatening note left behind on my car and said nothing more. Just to be here by 9am. It was now 8:51. I hated being late. I approached the front desk and explained my reason for visiting to the officer at the desk. He told me to have a seat in the waiting room, which was just down the hall.

The waiting room was empty and quiet, so I scrolled through my phone until Matt came out to get me. "This way Ms. Jones." Oh boy. I followed obediently behind, down a hall, to an office at the very end. The office was not very big, and had little in the way of furniture, except a large desk with two chairs in front and two more chairs stuck in the corner of the room beside a large file cabinet. Some photos and awards decorated the walls, but otherwise, the walls were bare. "Have a seat." Matt motioned towards the chairs in front of his desk. He sat in the big leather chair behind his desk and pulled out a notebook and pen, ready to take notes, I suppose. This was definitely not a friendly chat, and this was not the same man that had picked me up after work in his cruiser the other day to ask a few questions. Nope. This was an "I mean business" detective that I sat in front of, and although I was rather nervous, I was also somewhat perturbed at his icy demeanor. Had I done something wrong? Was I suddenly a suspect in Bob's death investigation? I couldn't see how that was possible, but I certainly wasn't feeling any warm fuzzies today.

Matt opened his desk drawer and pulled out a clear bag with a piece of paper inside, and set it on the desk in front of me. "Is this the note you found on your car yesterday?" I sat forward to get a closer look at the writing.

"Yes, it appears to be. I gave it to the officer yesterday when I filed the report about my slashed car tire."

"Tell me about that day, please."

"Pretty straightforward, really. I already told the officer that took the report. I went outside on Monday morning to go to the grocery store, but when I got to my car, which was parked in my driveway, I noticed my tire was flat. And I found the note tucked under my wiper on my windshield. I took a photo of my flat tire and the note over to Harry's and he drove me here to file a report." I sat back in my chair with my arms crossed. Matt was definitely giving off some negative vibes. I had always picked up on stuff like that. It was making me uncomfortable.

"What were you doing right before you went outside?"

"I was going to bake a French Apple Cake from my grandma's old recipe book but realized I was missing some ingredients. Well, most of them actually, but that's besides the point. Thing is, I needed to figure out which recipe I was going to use for the Blueberry Falls bake-off that I promised Angela I would enter. Angela is away next weekend and wanted the bookstore represented." I tended to ramble whenever I was nervous. Not sure why, but I would end up going on and on about the most trivial things. Today was apparently no exception. Looking up, I noticed Matt's tight, unsmiling expression. He appeared frustrated, actually.

"Alright Ms. Jones! I get it. You were baking. Please stick to relevant information."

"But you asked what I was doing before I went outside. I was trying to tell you." I knew darned well I was being facetious, but Matt, or actually, Detective Calhoon, was being an ass. He was acting like he had never met me. Like we had never sat and talked in his cruiser. Like I hadn't helped him find the perfect books for his niece. And like there had been no spark at all on any previous encounters. So ya, I was a little irked and I guess I should have behaved better, but I couldn't help myself.

Matt held his hand up to stop me from continuing. "Okay, I get it. Do you know who left the threatening note? And why?"

I shook my head back and forth. "I have no idea who left the note, or why someone would have slashed my tire." I lied. I didn't know, but I did have one idea. I thought it might be Eddie Caldwell. I wanted to tell Matt about our visit to Eddie's the other day. And the information Harry had told me. Which I would assume Matt would already have access to. Seeing that Harry got it from his old partner. But I wasn't sure now was the best time, with his prickly demeanor and all.

"So you have no idea who would threaten you to stay out of their business? I find that hard to believe, Ms. Jones. And don't bother denying that you and Harry have been snooping around in our investigation of Bob Filmore's death. Because I know you have. So you might as well tell me what you and our old friend Harry Lufkin have been up to before I charge you with impeding an active investigation. I have heard from several sources that you have been snooping around in people's business and I must say, Ms. Jones, that as a newcomer to our town, nosey snoops aren't generally liked. You and Harry have ruffled some feathers. So, spill it." Matt's voice was like a low rumble that reminded me of when my dad would get furious at us kids for something. Perhaps I should drop my attitude and tell him what we had found out so far. I just wish he would drop his attitude too, because it would make it a whole lot easier to share information with a friendly face than his scowling one.

Before I began, I took a deep breath. "Well, Harry found out that Ellen Caldwell's ex-husband was living out on his Uncle Gus' old farm and thought it would be a good idea to go talk to him. Just to ask him a few questions is all. Harry said that Eddie had a temper and had recently got out of jail. He also thought Eddie might have heard some things around town, because Eddie and his family know all the locals, and usually were among the first to hear about things."

"Okay, go on." Matt sat with his pen poised over his notebook, ready for some juicy tidbit of information from me.

"We didn't actually get anything worth mentioning because Eddie suddenly changed his mind about talking to us that day and told us to leave. Which we did."

"So you are saying he was going to talk to you, but then suddenly decided not to? Why would he do that?"

"Ummm, well, ..." I debated telling him about mentioning his ex-wife's affair with Bob but decided I needed to come clean and tell him everything we had learned so far, even if it meant putting my new friend Ellen on the suspect list. If she wasn't already on it. "Harry asked Eddie about Ellen and Bob's affair, to see his reaction, because we weren't sure if it was true or not at that point. That's when Eddie told us to leave."

"Wait a minute! Back up. What have you heard about an affair? Who told you that Bob Filmore and Ellen Caldwell were having an affair? And how long have you known? Oh, and one more question to add. When were you planning to tell me about this important piece of information?" Matt's face had turned a slightly darker shade of red from when we started out. I wanted to tell him to watch his blood pressure, but now was probably not the best time.

"First of all, Harry had only heard about the affair through the Blueberry Falls gossip hotline, so we weren't even sure that there was any truth to it when we went to see Eddie. However, gauging by Eddie's reaction, I kinda figured there was something to it. So I decided to investigate a little further and go right to the source. You know, get it directly from the horse's mouth, so to speak?

Isn't that what country people say?" I tried smiling at Matt now, knowing I was likely digging myself down further with every extra word I said at this point. He did not respond in kind, but sat quietly, waiting for me to continue. His face was now unreadable. He scribbled some things in his notebook, then stopped and waited. I took it as my cue to continue. "I decided to pay Ellen Caldwell a visit after work one day and ask her directly. She admitted that her and Bob were having an affair for the last year. She also told me that Bob had broken it off with her a few days before he died. Apparently he was fixing things with his wife Victoria and no longer wanted to see Ellen." There, I had said it. I sat back in my chair, feeling rather drained. And also feeling guilty for exposing Ellen and Bob's affair, because I knew this would put her at the top of the suspect list, and although I understood that this now gave her an excellent motive to kill Bob, I really didn't think Ellen Caldwell was a cold-blooded murderer. My cocky attitude had now disappeared and was replaced with a feeling of dread. I had exposed Ellen's secret. That wasn't something I was proud of. But it most certainly was relevant in this case.

Matt's voice was softer now. Less threatening and police-like. "Is there anything else you and Harry have learned while snooping into Bob's death?" I filled Matt in on everything else I could remember. I told him about Ellen's encounter with Marty and the fact that her son

Nathan drove a black pickup truck, and that I saw a black truck pull away as soon as I had arrived at Ellen's that day I dropped in for a visit. I even mentioned the FOR SALE sign on the Filmore's lawn and that Harry thought it was strange they would sell their home, when Bob had told him how much he loved that house. After I finished recalling everything, Matt and I had both relaxed. I had rid myself of my defensive attitude, and Matt was no longer acting like a cold stranger while we chatted. I stood up to leave, but Matt stopped me.

"Wait Sydney. Before you go. If you could give your best guess at who slashed your tire, who would it be?"

"Eddie Caldwell." I stated without even considering my answer.

"You need to be careful. And you and Harry both need to leave the investigating to the police. I realize you aren't breaking any laws. Yet. But you are obviously stirring up some trouble or you wouldn't be getting threatening notes. Whoever sent that note and slashed your tire means business. Take this seriously, Sydney. You could be in danger. So could Harry. And it could be the same person who killed Bob." Matt paused to make sure I was paying attention. I was. "Maybe I should assign someone to keep an eye on you and your house. Just to be safe."

"No way! I don't want some cop following me and checking up on me all the time. That's the last thing I need. If I was having issues meeting new friends before, that would be sure to help keep everyone away. I am fine. I can take care of myself. Besides. Harry and I went and bought some security cameras for the front of my house. He said he would help me install them this week."

"I can't force you to accept my protection. But promise me you will stay out of this." I would not make a promise I knew I wouldn't keep, so I said nothing in reply as I walked out the door and left the station. I needed to go talk to Harry so we could figure out our next steps.

Chapter 13

My day at the bookshop started out fairly quiet. It was a dismal, rainy Wednesday morning, and I didn't expect too many customers to be venturing out. So, Angela and I decided it was a good time to reorganize some of the back shelves and clean up the book club room area. I didn't mind doing it at all, because we always chatted and sipped on tea while we worked. This morning was no exception. The previous night, we had the Tuesday book club meeting, and there was a bit of a mess left to clean up from it. Last night's meeting hadn't gone quite as planned and Angela and I had shut it down early, ushering everyone out quicker than usual in order to avoid any trouble. As we tidied up the room and cleaned up the dishes, I thought about how thankful I was that I hadn't been hosting the book club alone last night. Although it had started out like every other one I had attended so far, there were a couple of interesting events.

The chosen book of the month was an older mystery, but it was good. Sue Grafton's book "T is for Trespass." And everyone seemed to have liked it because it was one of the best book club turn outs so far. I counted sixteen people gathered around the room last night. Among them were some bowlers that I recognized, including Frank and Nancy Marshall, Sara-Lynn Mitchell and George, the gossip. I couldn't recall his last name, but always remembered how Harry had described him. Usually, Angela had a set of questions that she prepared prior to the meetings to help get the discussions rolling. For this week, she had asked me to help prepare them because she had been busy getting everything ready to go away for her great niece's wedding on the weekend. She planned to leave on Friday morning for the trip and to be back by Monday. A past employee of Angela's, Harvey Reynolds, was coming to work at the bookstore to cover for Angela and me on Friday and Saturday. That way, I could concentrate on the bake-off. I was already feeling nervous about it. Throughout high school, Harvey had worked for her during summer breaks, but then left when he started college. He was back in town for a couple of weeks to visit his family and said he'd love to work a couple of days to cover for Angela. He was coming in on Thursday during my afternoon shift to catch up on anything that might have changed since he had left. I was relieved because I was really feeling the pressure to do well at the fair. I was representing the bookshop, after all. And I didn't want to embarrass myself in my first ever baking competition in my new hometown.

As we tidied up the back room, my mind wandered back to the book club meeting. Angela would ask questions and everyone would take turns answering. That's the way it was supposed to go anyway, but somehow, the topic of Bob's death was brought up repeatedly. He was on everyone's mind, which was not too surprising, since most locals knew him. Angela tried hard to keep everyone on track but was unsuccessful, so people kept going back to the topic of Bob's death, and the possibility that it was a murder. And much of the turn of discussion was attributed to George, who would constantly blurt out something random that got everyone talking all at once. He kept stirring everyone up, and it was frustrating.

"I hear the police might not believe it's an accident." George stated, while looking around the room for some sort of confirmation. "Has anyone else heard anything about it?" His gaze rested directly on me then, but I looked down at my copy of the book and began flipping through pages.

"I heard something about that too!" the usually quiet and shy Sara-Lynn piped in. She sat forward in her chair, looking ready to stand. "I heard they think it was a Blueberry Falls local that might have done it." Everyone turned to look at Sara-Lynn, waiting for her to continue sharing what she knew. Her face went several shades of red with the attention and she slid back down in her chair, with the brief burst of confidence already lost. "That's all I heard, though. No one told me who they thought might have done it. I don't know anything else about it."

"Well, I am pretty sure that Bob was having an affair." George added confidently. "I also heard that Bob's wife Victoria found out about it and that's why they were selling their house. They were going to get a divorce and Victoria was planning to leave town and start over." The look of satisfaction on George's face made him look like a grinning cat that had just caught a mouse. All satisfied and proud of himself.

At that moment, I decided I didn't like George much at all and would avoid any further interaction with him, because he was a terrible gossip that didn't seem to care about anybody's feelings, as long as he was the one sharing all the juicy tidbits of information, true or untrue. Harry had warned me about him. And my mother had always warned me to stay away from people like that. I could hear my mother's voice saying, "Sydney, avoid people who gossip about others; they'll gossip about you, too." Her warnings had stuck with me through the years, but I hadn't really known anyone that gossiped much. Until now, with George.

"What!? Who on earth did you hear that from? I cannot imagine Bob Filmore ever stepping out on his lovely wife, Victoria. That can't be true." Nancy Marshall had been friends with the Filmores for years. "Victoria has been with our quilting group for years. We meet every week, and she's never said one word about anything being wrong. I am positive I would have known about it if she knew about it." Nancy's husband Frank put his hand on her arm to calm her, and she sat back down again, but the entire mood in the room had turned tense. Everyone seemed on edge.

"I don't know who the affair was with, but pretty sure it was some local that hung around the bowling alley. I got my information from a reliable source, so I'm pretty sure it's correct." George bragged.

"Okay, let's get back to the questions about our book, shall we?" Angela was tiny, but Blueberry Falls considered her an authority figure, so everyone nodded and we returned to discussing the book seriously.

I tried to put last night's heated discussion to rest and concentrate on the task at hand. When we had finished sorting shelves, unpacking boxes and straightening the room back to order, Angela and I both sat down for a rest. There hadn't been one customer so far the entire morning, but I could hear the rain pouring down on the roof, so I imagined people weren't too keen on stepping outside if they didn't have to. We took advantage of the quiet time and made some tea while we went over what Angela had planned for her weekend away and my weekend at the fair.

I was thankful that Angela avoided mentioning Bob's death, but it didn't surprise me. After last night's tense talks, neither one of us was too keen on talking more about town gossip. A few customers finally came in once the rain let up, and after they left, Angela left to run some last-minute errands before the weekend. I sat on the stool behind the counter, staring out the window, watching as people tried to navigate around the puddles in the street. When my phone rang, I just about fell off the stool in surprise.

"Sydney, it's Ellen." Her voice sounded a bit panicked. "Do you have a minute to talk? I know you are probably at work, but it's really important."

"There's no one in the store right now, so it's a good time. What's wrong?"

"I just got a call from Detective Calhoon and he has asked me to come down to the station for questioning. He said I can come voluntarily or he can send someone to pick me up! I'm about ready to throw up, Syd! What should I do?"

"Okay, the first thing you should do is just calm down. I am sure he is calling in lots of people to question them about Bob's death. It is an investigation. And you were there at the alley at the time we found Bob's body, so I'm not surprised."

"I know. I know. It's just that every time I try to talk about it, I panic or start bawling and I don't want to do either. I don't even want to think about this anymore. The whole thing is so awful. It's a nightmare."

"Ellen, you need to stay focused and just do as Detective Calhoon asked. What time did he ask you to be there?"

"I was told to be there between three and four today. Do you think you can come with me?" I looked at my watch. It was already almost one thirty. I didn't get off work until three and besides, Angela wasn't even here right now.

"I can't get away from work right now. If you'd like, I'm free to meet you there after three. But I'm not sure how much help I will be. They probably won't let me in the room when they question you, anyway." I couldn't hear anything on the line. "Ellen? Are you still there?"

"Yes, I'm here. Please come when you can, Syd. I could sure use your support."

"Of course. I'll drive there right from work. Look, Ellen, if you have nothing to hide and just tell them the truth, everything will be okay. See you shortly." I hung up and went back to staring out the window until Angela returned. I explained I had to run as soon as my shift was over. She told me I might as well go because there had only been a couple of customers the entire day, anyway. So I rushed off to meet Ellen at the police station.

I found her sitting alone in the waiting room. When I walked in, she jumped up to hug me. "Thank Gawd you're here. Oh boy, I was so worried you wouldn't get here before I was called in for questions." Ellen gripped my hand as we sat in silence, waiting. When Matt came out to bring her to his office, the look on his face at seeing me sitting holding Ellen's hand was definitely not one that said he was pleased about it. In fact, he scowled at me and told me I might as well go home because they could be awhile, and that there was absolutely no use in waiting around. Then he told one officer to make sure that I had left. Wow, he was steaming mad. I gave Ellen's hand a squeeze and told her she would be fine, then went straight to my car and called Harry on my way home. We made a plan to meet the next morning and go over everything we had learned so far. I picked up a takeout dinner on my way home and spent the rest of the evening watching romance movies and eating popcorn to help clear my mind.

Chapter 14

Harry and I were going to plan out our day over coffee at 10 a.m. He wanted to spend the day visiting potential suspects, and because I wasn't scheduled to work at the bookshop, we had plenty of time today. Eddie was first on our list.

I wanted to finish setting up my office before meeting with Harry, so I got up early and padded down to my kitchen to make coffee. Priorities. There were only two or three boxes left to unpack, and those were mainly books to put on the bookcase that I had bought the week before. It was my attempt at making my new house feel like home, but it was a slow process. I had to admit, I felt slightly more settled and less homesick than upon my arrival, but that might have been partly because my focus was on helping Harry solve Bob's death.

Lately, I had also been preoccupied with the story that had been kicking around in my head, and I wanted to sit down to do some writing, which meant finishing my office set up. It had been a very long time since I had written anything other than a few articles for local newspapers and magazines over the years, which was not the same as writing a fictional novel. That had been a dream of mine ever since I could remember. For so many years, I had set that dream aside for work and for my family. After that, I just lost the urge mostly, but it still lingered in the back of my mind. Always. Recently, the urge to write had grown, and a story began taking shape in my head. So now I wanted to properly set up my office and stop making excuses for not writing. Procrastination was a game I played well. And putting my dreams on hold to help my husband build his business. My dedication and loyalty to Gerard and his dreams apparently meant little to him, and I knew I had to come to terms with that fact. Somehow. I don't know when the tears began, but by the time I noticed I was crying, both my cheeks were wet. Dammit. I reached for a tissue and straightened my shoulders. Yes, he had betrayed me, but I needed to get over it and move on. I had loved Gerard. For years. Still did, I think. "Look where that got me. Nothing but heartbreak." Talking to myself was becoming a regular thing. I had to stop wishing things were different and accept that I was now a divorced woman of forty-six. Now I had freedom. And choices. And a new house. I wished I could get excited about it and stop feeling homesick. It was the cutest little bungalow. But I wished I wasn't alone. Even if Posh lived closer, it would help. Being alone was hard after spending half your life with a partner. It was too quiet here. Maybe I needed a pet. Maybe a dog. I had been considering getting a dog, so I didn't feel like I was talking to myself so much. After all, I had the room for one here. I had a big backyard that was surrounded by a five-foot wooden fence. The previous owners must have had dogs, because there was even a nice big doghouse in the back corner of the yard, under a giant oak tree. When I first arrived, I had checked it out. Someone had insulated it and added a cute little wooden platform outside the entrance for the dog to lie on. Throughout my childhood, I had always had multiple dogs. Gerard and I had a lovely little border collie puppy. We named her Madeline. Maddie for short. She was so smart and full of energy, and she kept us on our toes through the years. After she died, fifteen years later, Gerard said no more dogs. I had wanted another one almost immediately after we lost Maddie to help fill the giant hole her absence made. I had been feeling lonely after Posh went off to University in Ottawa and a new dog would have been good company since Gerard worked such long hours and was often away on overnights. But he was adamant, and I didn't feel like arguing over it with him, so we didn't get another one. Maybe it was time I got a dog. After all, I could certainly use the company during the long, dark nights that would soon be upon us. It was the end of September, and the days were getting shorter already. I slid the last book from the last box onto the bookshelf and stood back to admire my work. It was a good start, I thought, as I turned to finish getting ready for my day with Harry.

***

Eddie's pickup truck was in the drive when we pulled in. I couldn't help but wonder if his was the truck we saw that day pulling out of the alley. But his son, Nathan, had one too. So did Matt Calhoon, come to think of it. As I quickly learned, finding the owner of that specific black pickup without more information first was not likely in Blueberry Falls. I wish I had got a better look at the truck and the driver so I could point out something unique. I watched the horses gazing in the fields along both sides of the long driveway. It felt so peaceful. There weren't any other houses in sight, and no vehicles driving past the property. Checking my cell phone, I also realized that I only had one bar showing, so reception would be spotty at best here.

We walked across the well-kept lawn, and I half expected Eddie to come out of the house threatening us again like last time, but he didn't. In fact, we made it all the way to the front door and heard nothing but crickets. I was feeling anxious as I looked around the remote property, while Harry knocked on the door. After all, we could very well be confronting a murderer face to face. One that had just left a threatening note and slashed my tire as a warning to mind my own business. I didn't know for sure that it was Eddie, but a lot pointed to him being the guilty one. Harry told me he didn't have a good alibi for the time of the murder and that his old partner also suspected that Eddie's motive was strong. I mean, isn't a jealous ex-husband pretty high on the motive list? I thought so anyway. Plus, there was the stuff Harry had told me about Eddie spending time in jail for assault after he had beaten up that man bad enough to warrant a hospital trip. Eddie was someone not afraid to carry out threats. That was clear to me. What were we thinking, coming here to confront him, with no one else knowing where we were? And why did I always have to be so stubborn and decide not to give Matt a heads up about our plans today? In my defense, the last time I saw Matt was in his office when he acted like a real jerk, so I really didn't feel like messaging him with anything at all. I knew he would be mad and say we had to stay out of police business. Now, I was second guessing myself. Even if I had just sent him a text, it would have been safer. Goor grief, I wasn't very smart sometimes. But even Harry said to hold off on messaging Matt, because he wanted to gather a bit more evidence first, in case we were way off base. His old partner friend hadn't pulled up anything recently about Eddie. And even said that Eddie's parole officer had stated Eddie was doing well, keeping clean and sober, and hadn't missed a meeting with him. Eddie had a motive, though. He had told his parole officer that he was still in love with his ex-wife, Ellen. And that was cause for concern, because Bob and Ellen had been having a secret affair. Maybe it wasn't so secret after all. Another thing was that Eddie didn't have an alibi for the time of Bob's death. Apparently, he told the police he had been working in his barn at the time of the murder. He just couldn't prove it.

I must admit, when Harry first asked me to help him solve the mystery of Bob's death, I still believed that it may have been an accident. Even if it was an argument that had got out of hand or something. But I really didn't believe it was an intentional murder. I mean, this was Blueberry Falls. Things like murder didn't happen in places like this, did they? But I did believe Harry was experienced in homicide investigations, and he had suspected something was wrong all along. My beliefs had changed since we began uncovering secrets, investigating suspects, and gathering evidence. And ever since I had received the nasty tire slashing and the threatening note, I knew we were on to something. Now, I was certain Bob's death was no accident. Aside from knowing that Harry had a lifetime of training and practical experience, and I didn't see him as someone that jumped to conclusions without cause, I also understood that Bob was a long-time friend of Harry's, so I felt obligated to help him when he asked. And then, there was also my overly curious nature where I had, in the past, snooped into things that didn't seem quite right, and had, in fact, been correct in following my gut on most of those occasions. Once, I had solved a string of thefts in our neighborhood, and another time, I had actually led the police to an actual murderer. Gerard had been so upset with me. He claimed he was worried I would get hurt. I wondered if he was more worried about his reputation than about my safety. He said it would look bad to have his wife nosing around where it didn't belong and thought it might affect his business relationships somehow. Ultimately, people forgave my snooping because the capture of the real criminals brought them relief.

Harry knocked hard on the door. Sounded like a typical 'police knock' I imagined. It's how they always did it in movies, anyway. I grinned at Harry. He stood tall and alert. Still a cop at heart, even now, in his early seventies. I bet he still missed his job. He knocked a few more times while I tried to peek through windows. I didn't see any movement inside.

"Maybe he's in the barn working. Let's go check." The barn doors were closed, and I didn't hear any noise of tools coming from inside.

"Eddie, it's Harry. Are you in here? We're coming in to ask you a couple more questions, okay?" Silence. Harry slid the big wooden barn door open. There was a light on over the workbench and it looked as if Eddie might have been here working recently, but we couldn't see him from the doorway, so we went inside. Harry called out again. "Hey Eddie. Are you in here?" A bright ray of sunlight poured through the open door, lighting up a good portion of the dim barn, and making the dust dance in the air, as it radiated across the room, splaying a fan shape of light over the old floorboards. The workbench was neat, with tools hung in their proper places. On the bench were parts of what I guessed to be a chainsaw, all lined up neatly. Likely Eddie's current work project for another client. I still didn't see Eddie. Behind me, I heard a soft thud, and I emitted a small squeak of surprise as I wheeled around quickly, arms raised, ready to defend myself. I was just about ready to jump out of my skin. "Oh, you scared me." I laughed and crouched down to pet a small black cat that came just close enough to reach my outstretched hand.

Harry laughed. "A little jumpy, are ya, Syd?"

"I guess I am," I admitted. "Not everyone has your experience with this." The cat took one last sniff of my hand, then turned and scrambled up a wooden post and disappeared into the loft above. I rose and brushed the dirt from my pants and turned my attention back to the task of locating Eddie. "If his truck is here, he can't have gotten too far." I reasoned as I checked the other end of the barn. There, laying in the corner of the barn on the floor, was Eddie, with a puddle of blood around his head. I gasped. "Harry." My throat was dry, and words were hard to get out. "Harry!" I tried again. Harry spun around. "I found

Eddie." I rushed to Eddie and kneeled down on the floor beside him, checking for a pulse. "Harry, he's still alive! Call 911! Tell them to send an ambulance. Hurry!" Eddie's eyes flickered open and shut as he fought to stay conscious. The side of his head had a huge gash, which was where all the blood appeared to be coming from. I remembered a roll of paper towels on a rack by the workbench, and quickly scrambled to grab them, hoping to slow the bleeding, while Harry gave the 911 operator the information. Pulling off a bunch of paper towels, I held them tightly to the gash on the side of Eddie's head. "Help is on the way, Eddie. Don't worry. The ambulance is coming soon." I reassured him, although I knew it might not be soon enough. We were over fifteen minutes from town, and the dirt roads were difficult to navigate at high speeds, so it could be awhile. Eddie struggled to keep his eyes open. They locked on mine. "You're going to be okay, Eddie." He reached for my free hand, while my other one held pressure on the paper towel bandage on his wound. I cradled his hand. "Who did this to you, Eddie?" He struggled to speak, and I couldn't make out the words.

"Ma……ma….mar." his hand let go of mine and fell to the floor, but his eyes held mine. His words were unintelligible to me. His voice was almost inaudible to me. I picked up his hand again, trying to comfort and reassure him, desperately hoping he wouldn't die right here beside me.

"Help is on the way. Hang on. Stay with me. You are going to be okay," I lied, reassuring him and myself, although I didn't really know whether or not that was true, given all the blood. Eddie's eyes shot wide open and bore right into mine. He tightened his hold on my hand.

"El. Not sssss. El……." Again, I struggled to make out what he was saying. Eddie's eyes closed and his arm dropped limp to the floor. I wasn't sure if he was unconscious or dead, but I kept reassuring him anyway.

"Help is on the way, Eddie. Soon. They will be here soon." There was no response at all. I looked up at Harry as he stood, staring back at me, still holding his phone in his hand.

Chapter 15

As I sat with Eddie, waiting for the ambulance to arrive, my mind raced. Who did this to Eddie? Was it the same person who had killed Bob? Did that mean that Eddie was not the murderer? And if Eddie didn't do it, then who did? I thought Eddie had slashed my tire and left me that threatening note. Now, I was doubtful. My stomach flipped, and I gasped. Maybe I was in much more danger than I first thought. Where the heck was the ambulance? How long had it been? Time was moving so slowly as I sat holding Eddie's hand. He was no longer trying to talk to me, but he squeezed my hand a bit when I told him that help was on the way. I hoped he would be okay, that the ambulance would get here in time. Although I initially thought that Eddie might have died when his arm had dropped to the floor, limp, the small rise and fall of his chest told me otherwise.

I looked over at Harry. "He's going to be okay, Syd." Harry's reassurance helped calm me. After Harry had finished giving the emergency operator the information they needed to send help, he quickly searched the barn to make sure no one was lurking in one of the empty stalls, or hiding up in the loft. Then he came over to help me with Eddie. There wasn't much either of us could do, but Harry stuffed his jacket under Eddie's head to keep it off the floorboards. I held the wad of paper towels to the gash in Eddie's head, which appeared to have helped with the bleeding. Now, we waited, and my mind raced through the scenarios of who could have done this to Eddie and how. I couldn't believe how my instincts had been so off about believing Eddie might have been the murderer. He could still be, I supposed, but it had become less likely given the circumstances. I looked around the barn. Someone had likely hit Eddie with the wooden 2x4 board that lay discarded about a dozen feet away. Neither Harry nor I had gone near the bloody board, so as not to disturb any evidence.

Finally, I heard the approaching sound of sirens and felt some instant relief. Harry went outside to meet them and show them where we were. If Eddie was okay, maybe he could tell us who did this to him and why, before it happened again. My mind ran over Eddie's attempts to talk to me before he passed out. What was he trying to say? It was something like *save something or safe*? He had been barely audible and mumbling so much that I really couldn't give a good guess. Could his mutterings of *el* have meant Ellen? Could he have been trying to tell me someone else was in danger? Was Ellen in danger? I would talk it over with Harry later. Maybe we could figure it out together. As

I relaxed, knowing help was almost here, I took a moment to scan the barn floor while I sat. The barn floor was actually much cleaner than I expected, and someone had swept it recently. A broom and shovel leaned against a garbage can in the corner near a workbench. It was smart practice to keep it swept regularly, I supposed, repairing small engines and such, so it would make it easier to find any escaped parts that may fall from the bench. So, as I looked around, it made it easy to spot the large shiny silver button laying on the floor about five or six feet away from me. I didn't think it looked like it belonged to any type of machinery that was in the barn. It looked like a button off of clothing. As I tried to get a better look, I thought that maybe I had seen something like it somewhere before. But where? I pulled my phone from my pocket with my free hand, being sure not to move my other hand that kept pressure on Eddie's head. I leaned towards the button and snapped a few photos, zooming in as close as possible. It wasn't the best angle, but hopefully I could get a couple more shots before emergency responders arrived. I also snapped some photos of the bloody wooden board before stuffing my phone back in my pocket. Then I resumed my scan of the barn floor while we waited. Just having something to focus on that I thought might be useful had a calming effect on me.

I looked down at Eddie. His eyes were still closed, and his chest still rose up and down. The barn doors opened, and Harry came rushing through, followed by two paramedics and police right behind them. "This way. He is over here in the corner." Harry directed the crew of responders towards Eddie and I. Relief flooded over me as they took over. But then I looked more closely at the accompanying police officers, and I realized I recognized them both from when we had found Bob's body, a few days prior.

The paramedics took over, and I went to stand beside Harry out of their way. I leaned in and whispered, "Harry, it's the same cops that were at the scene when we found Bob."

"I see that. It's not a big police department, so it's not surprising."

"Oh Gawd, they must be wondering how on earth both of us came to be at both scenes before anyone else." Harry merely nodded and shrugged his shoulders as we stepped back further to let them all do their jobs.

"Yep, and they may have a lot of questions for the both of us." Harry put his arm around me in comfort. "But don't worry. You did good, Syd. I think Eddie is going to be okay." I rested my head on his shoulder. Harry was becoming more than just my neighbor and friend. He sometimes felt like a father figure, and that was all right by me.

"Well, I must admit that I am relieved to see that Matt isn't with them today. After lecturing me the other day about interfering with a police investigation, I can just imagine how mad he would be if he saw us here right now."

"You know he will find out anyway, don't you? He is in charge at the station, so he will be involved, and most likely, following up with us both soon."

"I'm still glad he isn't here right now, because I don't think I could take his icy glares after everything that has happened." I was shivering although it wasn't cold outside. Harry wrapped his arm around me protectively.

"You did so good, Sydney. If it wasn't for us finding Eddie, I doubt he would have survived. Even now, I'm not so sure he will make it, but he sure as heck has a better chance because we found him." While the paramedics loaded Eddie into the ambulance, two officers came over to take our statements. I watched as Harry followed one outside of the barn. I followed the other officer to a bench under a beautiful apple tree about 20 yards from the barn doors. As the officer scribbled notes, I looked up and saw that Matt was walking directly towards us. I glanced over to where Harry sat answering questions, hoping he would catch my eyes. I was not up to another lecture from the detective. Still shaky, I only wanted to go home. Harry was nodding to the cop that had been taking his statement, then got up and headed in my direction, thankfully.

"Ms. Jones. We meet again. And again, you and your friend Harry just happened to be at the scene of a crime. Seems like an unlikely coincidence, doesn't it? Especially after I gave you explicit instructions to stay out of police business." Matt didn't wait for me to respond before he turned and addressed the cop that had been taking my statement. "If you have finished with Ms. Jones, you can go back and finish securing the scene." Then he looked directly at me. "I am sure these two have contaminated some of the evidence already." Matt waved his hand towards Harry and I. "You two need to go home now before you contaminate any more of the crime scene." Matt was abrupt and cold. I suddenly felt the heat rising in my cheeks. I was suddenly furious.

"Contaminate?! Are you kidding me?!" I was aware I was shouting at the police officer in charge, but I didn't care. "If it wasn't for us coming in when we did, Eddie Caldwell might not even be alive!" I stood, shaking and furious, directly in front of Matt.

"Harry, take Ms. Jones home, please. And I suppose I don't need to tell either of you we will need you for further questioning later." With that, the detective strode off towards the barn.

Harry gently grabbed my arm and steered me towards his car. "Come on Syd. Let's get out of here." Although I was still fuming and wanting to say more, I did what Harry asked.

Chapter 16

When I got home after finding Eddie in his barn, I was exhausted but too stressed to sleep. I did laundry and some other chores that I had been ignoring, but was still feeling too restless to sleep, so I decided to bake. Baking had always calmed my nerves in the past, and maybe it would help now. Two days before the bake-off, I wanted to practice the French Apple Cake one more time. I had a chamomile tea instead of coffee while I was baking, to help destress. I really didn't need any more caffeine today. As I pulled the ingredients and baking utensils out and sipped on my tea, I could feel the tension leaving already. This was exactly what I needed right now. The cake went into my oven, and I set the timer. I was relieved to realize that I didn't need to refer to the recipe once, so I felt confident I would be okay for the no recipe use rule in the contest.

I made another tea and sat down to flip through my grandma's recipe book for something else to make while I waited, but before I even got started, there was a knock on my door. "Who the heck can that be?" I asked myself. It was late and I rarely got visitors after dinner time. I looked through the window and saw Matt Calhoon standing on my porch. Maybe he has more questions for me about Eddie. Or maybe he was just here to give me another lecture about snooping around in police business. Either way, his presence didn't thrill me. He did look good, though. He must be off duty because he's not in his cop uniform, I thought as I opened my door.

"Hi Sydney. I hope this isn't a bad time, but I just wanted to give you an update about Eddie's condition, and to check in on you, to see how you were doing with everything that happened. Can I come in for a moment? I won't take up too much of your time."

I stood back to allow him passage. "Sure. I guess. But we will have to sit in the kitchen, because I am in the middle of baking, and I need to keep an eye on my cake in the oven."

Matt smiled. "Baking? I didn't know you were a baker."

"Well, how could you? You barely know me." I spoke more sharply than I intended, but I was still angry at him for how he treated me earlier. And the other day too. He was a real jerk, in fact. Even so, I hadn't intended on sounding rude. I continued. "I'm not really a baker. Sometimes, I enjoy baking. It relaxes me. And I had to practice making the cake that I am baking at the Blueberry Falls Main Street business bake-off on Saturday. Angela asked me to take her place in representing her bookshop because she's away at a wedding this weekend and didn't want the bookshop to miss a chance at the coveted trophy."

"Well, it certainly smells good." You smell good, I thought. Matt sat at the kitchen table, looking a little nervous. Not the same take-charge, bossy guy from earlier today. "What is it?"

"It's a French Apple Cake. You can be a taste tester if you want." I offered, although I wasn't sure why I was being so hospitable when I thought he was a jerk. A cute jerk. But still a jerk. On the way home from Eddie's, I had mentioned what I thought about Matt's gruff treatment to Harry, but he explained that Matt had done nothing but follow protocol at the scene. I wasn't sure why I expected him to treat me differently than he would any other person at a scene, but I did. Or I had hoped he would, anyway. It was just such a change from our comfortable conversation on the first day we had met at the bookstore. He was just a regular guy then. A nice guy shopping for a gift for his niece. I had no idea he was a cop. Not that it should make a difference, but it did, given the circumstances. A lot. Dammit. Why the heck should I care if he is a jerk? It's not like I have any interest in dating him, or anyone, for that matter, right now.

"Oh, I won't say no to that offer." Matt grinned at me. "I have a sweet tooth, and I am always a sucker for cake."

"How is Eddie doing?"

"He is stable now. Still unconscious, and the doctors said they are going to keep him in an induced coma state for the next twenty-four to forty-eight hours, because of some brain swelling. Head injuries can be tricky. They felt he should be fine, but he took quite a wallop to his head, and he might have some amnesia when he wakes up. We can't question him until he is fully awake, so it will be Saturday probably, before he can tell us anything about who attacked him."

"Thank goodness they say he will be okay. I was scared he might die for a while there." Thinking back to the scene and the blood, my hands shook, despite my intention not to be vulnerable in front of Matt. Because I didn't want him to notice, I held my cup tighter. "I'm sorry. I should have offered you a coffee or water or something. I'm having chamomile tea. What would you like?" I jumped up to busy myself at the counter.

"A tea would be great. I just finished a long shift, and I am pretty tired. You are my last stop of the night before I head home to get some shuteye. You know, today would throw anyone off Sydney. It was a lot." Matt looked straight into my eyes. His were a soft brown. I couldn't hold his stare and looked away. It was confusing. One minute, treating me like a suspect at a crime scene, or lecturing me about getting into his business, and next, sitting in my kitchen, drinking tea, and updating me about Eddie. "Harry said that if it wasn't for your quick first aid actions, Eddie might not have made it. So, you probably saved his life. That's really something Sydney." Matt paused for a moment, looking as if he was contemplating how to proceed. "When we arrived on scene, my job was to secure the scene as fast as possible and try to preserve any evidence that might be there. Protocol. I hope you can understand that." Matt didn't come right out and apologize for being such a jerk earlier, so I figured this was as close as he was going to get to it. I let my guard down a bit and forgave his earlier crustiness. After that, we chatted casually, while we waited for the cake to be done. My kitchen had a wonderful smell of apple cake and whatever cologne Matt was wearing. The mixture was calming, and I felt my body give in to relaxation. We had such a pleasant chat. I learned Matt had been single for the last six years, after he and his fiancé had a mutual breakup. They had been engaged for over three years, but each wanted different things, and once they realized they weren't the right fit as life partners, they broke up. She moved to the States, and he stayed in Blueberry Falls, the town where he grew up. He had run into her at a New Year's party last year and met her new husband. He thought the guy was perfect for her and seemed genuinely happy about it. I wish I could have the same ability to move forward in my life, but I wasn't there yet.

I told Matt about Gerard. I explained how ours was not such a friendly break-up. As I told him my story, I realized how cliché it sounded. But cliché or not, it was what had happened. It was my story. "Now, I am just trying to pick up the pieces and move on without feeling so sorry for myself." I explained. Then I laughed. "My daughter Posh is still so angry with him. She's barely spoken to him over the past two years, and I really wish they could mend things between them. When Posh was younger, those two were so close. At one time, Gerard was a great husband and father. Looking back, it's so hard to tell where it all fell apart."

"I didn't know you had a daughter." There he went again. I mean, how could he know that? Unless he had investigated me. Which he very well could have, given the circumstances. I had first been on the scene of two different violent crimes in less than two weeks, and I was new in town. If I were him, I would investigate me. I looked suspicious for sure.

"Yes, I have a daughter. Posh is twenty-two and lives in Ottawa. She recently graduated from university there. A journalism degree. She got a job right after she graduated. I am so proud of her, and relieved she found work so fast, even though I wish it had been closer to home." I couldn't help but smile while I told Matt about Posh. Finally, the timer buzzed, and the cake was ready. Both of us had a giant slice. The cake had turned out perfectly, and Matt was thrilled when I packed up half of it for him to take home. After he left, I made a quick call to Harry and updated him about Eddie's condition. Then we made a plan for the following day. I was tired and ready for bed by the time I finished cleaning up the kitchen, but still tossed and turned all night with dreams of Eddie lying unconscious in the barn.

Chapter 17

Harry and I had a full day of visiting, and sleuthing planned for the day. It had been eleven days since finding Bob's body, and we both felt no closer to finding the killer than when we started. I had been so sure Eddie was involved in Bob's death. That was, until we found him lying in a pool of his own blood in his barn, barely alive. Now I didn't know what lead to follow next. Neither did Harry. So we had come up with a plan to split up for the day and do some investigating on our own. Harry was going to go see Victoria again, hoping to find out more about the affair and what she knew about it. Blueberry Falls was a small town, and it was highly unlikely that Victoria hadn't at least heard a few rumors about Bob and Ellen by now. Harry also wanted to ask about the house being up for sale. He thought she might be more likely to discuss things with him without everyone else being there, like the last time we went to see her. Next, Harry planned to meet George at Sally's Cafe for lunch and see what bits of gossip George had learned over the last week. Although his information may not all be accurate, it would certainly give us some more leads to follow up on.

My plan was to stop and visit Ellen and her son Nathan before they headed off to the hospital to sit with Eddie. Eddie was still in a coma. Apparently, Ellen and Nathan had been spending all their free time there, sitting at his bedside, waiting for him to wake up. Ellen clearly still cared a great deal for her ex-husband and Nathan was also close to his dad. Beside me on the front seat of my car was a freshly baked blueberry crumble to drop off at Ellen's place. Ever since stocking my cupboards with fresh baking ingredients, I had been on a baking spree and I was loving it. It felt good to be using my kitchen and baking had always been such a great de-stressor for me.

I walked up to Ellen's door armed with my blueberry crumble, but before I could knock, the door opened and Nathan's startled face greeted me. "Oh hey, Nathan. Sorry to surprise you like this. I just wanted to drop off some sweets for you and your mom." Nathan smiled and took the dish from my hand.

"Thanks Sydney. I love desserts and so does my mom. She's just running around trying to find her keys so we can head to the hospital and see dad. We are really hoping the doctors have some good news today and will bring him out of his induced coma." Just then, I heard Ellen call out from the hallway.

"I found them! Let's get going, Nate." Ellen stopped and looked at me as she rounded the corner. "Oh

Sydney. What a delightful surprise." She took the blueberry crumble from Nate's hands and set it on the stand beside the door. "That's so thoughtful of you to bring this for us. I'm sorry, I don't have time for a visit, because Nate and I are off to the hospital. The doctor wants to update us this morning on Eddie's progress and let us know when they will bring him out of his induced coma."

"Ellen, I understand completely. I only wanted to stop by quickly to give you the dessert and see how you are doing. I hope the doctor has good news for you today. Call me later if you can, okay?" I waved goodbye and rushed back out to my car to head to my next destination, which was Sandra Watt's farm.

Before backing out of my Ellen's driveway, I quickly checked my phone to study the directions to Sandra's place. It looked easy enough to get to, but Harry had told me the cell reception was spotty at best out there, so I figured I would go off the directions in my head instead of relying on GPS. I was learning not to rely too heavily on my car's GPS because it was often inaccurate on the Highlands back roads, or not available at all in some places that had no cell service.

Harry said it wasn't hard to spot Sandra's bright blue house once I was on her road, as it not only stood out, but was also only one of three houses on Jessup Lane, where she lived, along with her husband and two teenage boys. I just needed to keep my eye out for the tiny road sign on the right, shortly after the single lane bridge that crossed Jackson Creek.

The first part of the journey was familiar because it was the same road Harry and I had gone down when we went to Eddie's farm. The road was all dirt except for one short, paved section at the beginning, as I headed north out of town. I followed it along for a couple of kilometers, then turned right onto a side road. I'm not sure why I was feeling nervous. Maybe because I was heading into unfamiliar territory, but that seemed to be the story of my life lately. New town. New friends. New job. All of it was unknown territory. My recent divorce had shaken my confidence. So much so that I found myself having panic attacks when trying to do the simplest of things. It was frustrating. I used to feel so in control and brave. I loved being a wife and a mom to Posh.

Now, here I was, heart banging in my leaden chest, mouth so dry I needed to keep sipping water so as not to choke, and my palms sweaty on the steering wheel. "Stop it, Sydney!" I banged the steering wheel in frustration at my lack of self control, all because I had to drive down an unfamiliar road with little to no cell service. Geeze, I grew up before cell phones ever even existed. This was ridiculous. I was being ridiculous. How I had become this weak minded, anxiety riddled person, I don't know, but I knew I needed to change it, somehow? I missed my silly, brave, sometimes overly confident, old self. I missed my curious nature, although that had definitely returned a little since I had started helping Harry figure out what happened to Bob. And despite my trepidation, I was also glad that I had these snoopy tasks to occupy a good part of my brain lately.

I looked at my car clock. Sandra was expecting me at eleven and I was early, so I slowed down to take in some of the scenery. It really was beautiful out here. As I drove through an S bend in the road, I glimpsed a truck behind me in my rearview mirror. It was coming up fast behind me, so I slowed more and pulled close to the right side of the road, figuring it would just drive on past me. Instead, the truck pulled up close behind me and just followed along. "Well, okay, buddy. Have it your way and follow me, but I am not speeding up on these curvy roads." I know he couldn't hear me, but I thought he would get the message and pass on by once we hit the next straight stretch. The driver stayed behind. I could tell now that the truck was a dark color. Possibly black or really dark blue. And I could also tell that the driver was a male. Or at least I thought so. He had a red ball cap on, so I couldn't be sure. It was hard to see details for certain through my rearview. I was sure my slow driving must have frustrated the driver. Up ahead, I could see a narrow bridge and assumed it was the one that crossed Jackson Creek. The bridge looked quite old, and its sturdiness was questionable to me, but I crossed it without incident and I was relieved to see the sign for Sandra's road just ahead. Luckily, I would turn off, and the driver could be on his way without having to tailgate me much longer. Despite knowing he couldn't hear me, I yelled out my window. "Back off, buddy!" I assumed he was headed to the highway cutoff, which wasn't far past the bridge, if my map was correct. I turned down Jessup Lane, relieved to be off the other road. However, my relief was short-lived, because the darned truck turned right along with me, and still stuck right up close to the back of my car. If I had to stop fast, he would surely hit me, and maybe it wouldn't damage his big truck with the big steel grid attached to the front of it, but it would damage my little Civic. And it was only three years old. Gerard bought it for me about a year before we separated. It was his suggestion that I have a new car once Posh had headed off to university in Ottawa. I wonder now if maybe it was a guilt gift from him.

The truck was getting much too close for comfort, so I once again pulled to the right to allow the driver to pass. Again, he didn't. He stayed behind, so I pulled completely off the road and onto the shoulder to stop, but realized he was actually speeding up and aimed directly at me. Panicking, I quickly pulled back onto the road and sped up. The truck sped up too! My hands were sweating again as I gripped the wheel tightly. The guy sped up even more and was quickly closing the already small gap between us. "Oh, my God! He's going to ram me!" I slammed my foot on the gas to get away, but was too late. The impact of the truck jolted my head forward, and I almost hit the steering wheel with my forehead. I gripped the wheel and hit the gas hard, fishtailing down the dirt road to put some space between my little car and the truck. This guy was crazy! Why was he doing this? I reached for my phone on the passenger seat. Maybe I could get service and be able to call 911. My fingers could just touch the phone as I reached as far as I could, while still trying to stay on the narrow dirt road. Just as I grasped my phone, the truck rammed into the back of my car again, sending my phone flying to the floor and beyond my reach. I fought to keep my car on the road, but the next time he hit me from the left side, and I lost control. My car flew over a bank and down a hill, smashing into a tree. My body lurched forward hard. Luckily, the air bags deployed and stopped me from slamming into the steering wheel. The front of my car crumpled into the tree. The engine died and smoke rose from the hood. Stunned, I sat for a moment before realizing the danger I was in. I had to get out of my car. I shoved hard on my door, but it wouldn't open. Panic rose in my throat like a burning fire. I threw my left shoulder into the door as hard as I could and it finally opened enough for me to squeeze out. As I slid my feet out onto the ground, as could hear the crazy man's truck engine go roaring off. Breathing a sigh of relief that the crazy man had left the scene, I took in my surroundings. I was at the bottom of a hill about forty or fifty feet from the road. To put distance between myself and the smoking car, I pushed myself up, staggered away, and slumped onto the grass nearby, sobbing. I don't know how long I sat there before I heard voices above me at the top of the hill.

"Down here! Someone is down here! Call an ambulance! Hurry! I'm going down to help." I have no idea who owned the voice, but was thankful for it. Not a minute later, a large, beard-faced man in coveralls and a dirty brown cap kneeled in front of me. "Ma'am? Are you okay?" I nodded my head up and down in acknowledgement.

"I'm okay." I whispered. "A man. In a black truck. He rammed me off the road." I managed. "Call the police. He tried to kill me." I held back the well of tears I felt building. I suddenly felt nauseous and could feel the burn of bile rising in my throat. "Do you have any water?" I asked. "And my phone. I need it. It's on the floor in front of the passenger seat, I think. Can you find it for me, please? I need to call someone." I felt my senses coming back into focus as I sipped from the water bottle the giant man had handed me, but I could not contain my shaking hands. The man searched through my car, and returned with my phone, my purse and jacket. I hadn't even remembered any other items I might have needed from the car.

"I figured you'd need this other stuff, too." He waved the coat and purse. Smart thinking, I thought. "Here ya go." He handed my phone to me. "You won't be able to get any service down here, but if we can get you to the road, you should be able to make a call. Can you walk?" Just as the man asked, another guy came scrambling down the hill to help.

"Holy geeze!" he said. The second guy was much younger than the first, but they carried some resemblance. "You sure did a number on your car, lady. Are you okay?" Before waiting for my response, the young guy turned to address the older man. "Ambulance is on the way, dad. Cops too." I struggled to stand and, with the help of them both, I finally made it to the top of the hill. Although I was shaky and had a few bumps and cuts, I figured I would survive. My car, however, was a different story. It appeared to have met its end.

Chapter 18

It turned out that the two men that had come to my rescue were Sandra Watt's husband Harvey and one of their teenage sons. They pointed out a driveway less than a hundred feet from where we now stood and told me that Sandra would soon be down from the house with her van, so I could sit and wait for help to arrive. I called Harry and asked if he could come and pick me up once I could leave the scene and go home, seeing as I didn't have a vehicle now. Sandra arrived in her mini van shortly after and invited me to get in. She came armed with a large, heavy pink blanket, hot chocolate and water bottles. I slid into the passenger seat and accepted the blanket and hot chocolate with relief, as I was shivering profusely, presumably from the shock of the accident. I sat sipping hot chocolate and wrapped in the blanket that appeared to have been handmade. Likely by Sandra herself, I guessed.

As I sat and warmed up, the accident replayed in my head. Well, not accident at all, but an on purpose. An attempt at my life, I believed. As I relayed the events to Sandra, I cried, although I tried hard not to. I couldn't help myself. The whole thing had been terrifying, and I was realizing just how close I had been to being seriously hurt, or worse.

"Oh, my dear, that's just awful!" Sandra soothed, as she reached across the seat and pulled me in for a hug. I was not a huggy person, but I crumpled into a ball of tears in her caring embrace. "You're okay. There, there. You are safe now, Syd." I didn't feel safe. Not at all, actually. In fact, I felt the opposite of safe. My life was in danger. Someone had purposely run me off the road and left me down at the bottom of that hill, in a crumpled, smoking car. That someone had tried to kill me and I was scared. Sandra was probably the most motherly person I had ever met, and I thanked her for the support. Eventually, I pulled away and sat up in my seat, taking a long sip of the hot chocolate, and regained my composure. I was not usually so emotional, but this had shaken me; hard.

"Oh good, I can see flashing lights. Help has arrived." I watched through the window as a police cruiser and ambulance both arrived at the same time. I had seen a lot of flashing lights, cops and ambulances lately. More than my fair share. "You just wait right here, sweetie. I will let them know you are here warming up and send them over right away." I watched Sandra scurry across the road to the ambulance as she rushed over to inform the rescue team of my whereabouts. After a minute of them talking, and some hands pointing in my direction, Sandra seemed satisfied.

"They will be here in a jiffy," she informed me as she jumped back in the driver's seat to keep me company. Sandra's hot chocolate and gigantic warm blanket were working. I was feeling warmer than fifteen minutes ago, and my ability to think straight had improved, but my brain still felt foggy; like it was working in slow motion. My hands still shook, and my head was pounding as I sat sipping my drink. I also noticed that my left arm and shoulder were hurting quite a bit. Weird how I hadn't been aware of the pain until now. I searched through my purse and pulled out a bottle of Tylenol. Thank Gawd. I thought, as I popped two in my mouth. Hopefully, they kicked in soon.

I braced myself for more questions from the local police, but was surprised when I recognized Matt as the officer leaving the cruiser. "Oh, crap." I said under my breath. Sandra looked at me, then at where I was looking, and chuckled. Matt was talking to Sandra's husband and son. They pointed down the hill towards where my car was. Then they pointed towards Sandra's van. Matt headed towards us. My hands shook even more now, so I gripped the hot chocolate flask more tightly. It didn't help. I could see his frown from the other side of the road.

"He's okay, Sydney. Matt is one of our better veteran officers here in Blueberry Falls. He's a good guy. He's had a lot on his plate lately, with the big boss off the last few months from a heart attack. I heard from a reliable source that Matt is now in charge until the captain returns. I bet he's been awfully stressed." Sandra didn't realize that Matt had already warned me off the investigation last night and I hadn't told her that the reason I was coming to see her today was because I wanted to ask her some questions about Bob and the bowling league members. I had led her to believe it was just a friendly coffee visit. Matt would not be happy that I was, yet again, involved in a violent incident in his little town, after living here for less than four months. Nope. He was going to be angry that I was still nosing around his case. But all I could do was nod my head, because I couldn't explain it all to Sandra right now, anyway.

I opened the van door before he got to me and took a deep breath as I prepared myself for his angry lecture. "We meet again." He smiled, and my brow wrinkled in confusion. "I have questions, but first, I want the paramedics to check you over and make sure you are okay." I hadn't noticed at first, but the ambulance drivers were following right behind him, armed with equipment and wheeling a mobile bed. He crouched down in front of where I sat on the passenger seat and looked directly into my eyes. My heart skipped a beat. "You are okay, aren't you, Sydney?" His concern caught me off guard, and I fought back the tears that threatened to resurface at his gentleness. I nodded my head up and down, but was afraid to speak, for fear I would burst into tears again. Instead, I looked down and stared at my lap. He put his hands over both of mine, as they still gripped the warm thermos. "The guys that helped you up the hill told me that someone ran you off the road, then took off. They saw your car go over the bank and came running over to help. I'm so thankful they were here to help you. I have lots of questions for you but that can wait" Matt let go of my hands and stepped aside for the paramedics. He walked back over to talk to the two men again. The paramedics checked me over and suggested that I go with them to the hospital for a more thorough checkup. They were concerned with my pounding head and painful arm. I declined their offer and said I was fine and would wait for my friend to come and pick me up. Once the paramedics left, another officer came and took my statement, then told me someone would call me if they had further questions. He said Matt wanted to talk with me before I was free to leave. I was suddenly exhausted and just wanted to sleep, so I reclined my seat and closed my eyes while I waited. When Matt came back over to check in on me, the only questions he asked me were about the description of the driver. I gave him as much information as I could, but also explained that I had been so concerned with keeping my car on the road and escaping the guy and his giant truck I hadn't got a good look. I remembered the driver had a red ball cap sticking out from underneath a big dark colored hoodie, as an obvious attempt to disguise himself.

Finally, Harry arrived, so Matt walked me over to his car and opened the passenger door. I winced as I carefully slid into the seat. It was hurting more and more as time passed. "Are you sure you don't want to go to the hospital and have them check you over? The paramedics are still here and can get you there pretty quick. I'm sure Harry won't mind meeting you over there."

"No, I'll be fine. I think I just twisted it or banged it, or something. If it gets worse, I will go tomorrow. For now, I just want Harry to get me out of here. It's been an awful day. I am exhausted. And my car is totaled, so now I don't even know what I'm supposed to do." The tears came yet again. Frustrated, I swiped them away. Dammit, Sydney! Get a grip. You are being ridiculous. I chastised myself for being such a crybaby. Not like me at all. But then again, I had never had a day like this before. The shock of it was just setting in.

"Okay, Syd, you don't need to go to the hospital now, but I'm coming to check on you as soon as we're done here. That was quite the accident. I'm not even sure how you walked away from it, by the shape of your car." Matt then looked directly at Harry. "Take care of her,

Harry." It was more of a command than a request. "Seems that someone is pretty intent on doing Sydney some harm. She needs to stay with you at your place until I can get an officer to come by and keep watch over her."

"You got it, Matt."

"Hey, I'm right here guys!" Frustration instantly replaced my tears. "I just want to go home and have a nap. I don't want to go to Harry's. No offence, Harry, but I don't need a babysitter." I stated, far more boldly than I felt. I just wanted to go home and hide under the covers in my room right now. Not go to the hospital. Not go to Harry's. And not have some stranger cop hanging around, watching my every move. I knew it was to keep me safe, and I appreciated the effort, but it wasn't what I wanted right now, and I said so again. They didn't seem to care about my wishes.

"Frankly, Ms. Jones, I don't much care if you don't want someone watching out for you. You don't get a choice in the matter right now." Matt then turned to Harry. "Harry, she is to stay with you at your place until I am done here. Then I will be out to see you both. Understand?"

"You got it, Matt." Harry agreed with Matt, and it seemed I did not get a vote on the matter.

The first part of the drive home was quiet. Harry kept his eyes focused on the road while I steamed beside him. Eventually, he reached over and lay his hand over mine. "I'm so glad you are okay, girl. You have become quite a fixture in my life lately, and I don't know what I would do if something worse than today happened to you. I kinda need ya, Syd. Don't be mad at me and Matt. He's just trying to keep you safe, and so am I." Harry was right. I knew that. And besides, I don't think I could stay mad at Harry for long at all. I relied on, and cared about my tough old neighbor far more than I had realized.

"I'm not mad, Harry. Really. This whole thing has been so awful. It was terrifying. I mean, the guy was trying to kill me. Or at least hurt me really bad. And as much as I just want to run and hide in a hole right now, I also want to figure out who it was. Because I'm sure it has something to do with Bob's death. And I think they don't want me snooping around about it anymore. Thing is, as much as I am scared, I am also stubborn, and I need to figure this out."

"You, my dear, are like a dog with a bone. I know I asked you to help me find out what happened to my friend, but I didn't intend for you to get hurt. I am so sorry. Asking you to snoop around in other people's business was a mistake. I should have known better. I'm afraid I have made things even harder for you to be accepted by the locals than it should have been. You are brand new to this town, and people here are already wary of outsiders, even without them snooping around. And add a suspicious death in the mix, and the whole thing has turned into a big mess."

"Harry. It is not your fault. And besides, I could have said no to you, but I didn't. A part of me was actually excited to help you figure this out. It made me remember the way I used to be before I became such an anxious person. All this investigating stuff has been good for me. Well, until today, of course. And my tire being slashed. That wasn't so good either." I laughed. Harry laughed too. "Now, let's go over what we know so far. See if we can figure this thing out before something else happens. Okay?" Harry shook his head and smiled.

"You are one tough cookie, girl. Okay. Let's figure this out. Tell me everything you remember about the truck and the driver. We will go from there." After relaying the entire story, starting from where I noticed the truck was following too close behind me, to where I plunged over the side of the bank and smashed into the tree, crumpling my car. Then I proceeded to cry again. I think this was the fourth or fifth time today. Crap. I hated crying because it embarrassed me. Although I had no issue with others crying, and usually tried hard to comfort them, my upbringing taught me to suppress my own emotions. You know, the old, "stop crying, or I'll give you something to really cry about." So today was a rarity for me. But, in my defense, today's events were a rarity for pretty much anyone. When I looked over at Harry, the only thing I saw was concern. He reached over and squeezed my hand. "You are okay, Syd. You are safe and we will figure this out. Matt will be over later, and he will make sure you are safe." Harry's attempt at reassurance was helpful. However, it wouldn't help me with my crumpled car.

"But my car Harry! It's totaled. Gone. And now I can't even get to the bake-off tomorrow! I promised Angela, and besides, I was actually looking forward to it after I figured out what I was going to bake." The words just poured out, as I went on about the fair, and baking, and next, I was reminiscing about baking with my grandma. Harry didn't interrupt me. He just let me ramble on about the darned bake-off and about not having a car anymore, and now being stranded in a town where there wasn't even a bus service to help me get around.

Finally, when I was all done rambling, Harry said, "You can borrow my car tomorrow to get yourself to the fair, so don't worry about that. And first thing Monday morning, I will drive you to the car rental place in Huntsville, and you can get a rental until your insurance sorts stuff out for you. It's not the end of the world, Sydney." Harry made it all sound so easy peasy. And I suppose it really was. After all, people are in car accidents every single day, and they can figure it out. But I had never been in an accident, so it was completely new to me. I was so thankful for Harry, and told him so, as I reached across the seat and gave him a quick hug. He smiled but kept both hands on the wheel and had to shrug me off as we entered a big curve in the road. "I'm sure George will take me over to the fair later in the day so I can help you pack up your stuff and hopefully sample some of the delicious bake-off entries." How did I ever get so lucky to have a neighbor like Harry?

Chapter 19

I woke up early the next morning and lay in my bed thinking about the terrifying events of the previous day. Harry had walked me home and tucked me in late last night. I remember dozing off on his couch until he nudged me awake, saying I would be more comfortable in my bed, which was very true, as Harry's couch isn't all that comfortable. I also remember him saying that Matt would drop by early this morning to check on me because I was sleeping when he dropped in at Harry's last night after finishing up at the crime scene. Although I didn't feel that he needed to be checking in on me, I was eager to hear any updates about Eddie's condition.

It was 6:15 am. Time to get moving. I knew I had lots to prepare before leaving for the bake-off, but when I rolled over to get out of bed, I let out a loud screech. "Oh, my Gawd! How am I so sore?" I realized that my entire body was screaming at me. It felt like a Mack truck had hit me. When I moved my left arm, pain shot right up through my shoulder. I sat back against the pillow as my head pounded, too. How on earth was I going to get through the bake-off today when I couldn't even get out of bed? I needed to get some Tylenol into me, and fast, if I was going to have any chance at all today. Slowly, I maneuvered myself around until I sat up with my feet on the floor and forced myself up. "Don't be a baby, Syd. Move it." When I was finally up, I shuffled down to the kitchen and swallowed a couple of Tylenol, and Advil, too. I needed both for sure. Then I headed to stand under a steaming shower for the next fifteen minutes. By the time I was dressed and back in the kitchen making coffee, I could move around slightly better. Relieved, I sat down to go over the list of items I needed to bring to the fair for the bake-off. Thankfully, there wasn't much, because they supplied all the baking ingredients at the contest.

As I drank my second cup of coffee and waited for life to return to my body, I scrolled aimlessly through my phone photos. I had been taking a lot of pictures lately but hadn't had a chance to go through them all yet. As I was scrolling, I stopped on the photos I took in Eddie's barn. With everything that happened yesterday, I had forgotten about these. I had a couple of photos of the bloody board that was the likely weapon, and I had three photos of the big silver button that had been lying on the barn floor. I zoomed in for a closer look. As I studied it, I wracked my brain for where I had seen it before, or one very similar at least, but couldn't place it. I wondered if the detectives had figured anything out about it yet, or if they even thought it was relevant to Eddie's attack. My doorbell chimed, and I glanced up at the clock. I slowly rose from my chair and made my way, painfully, I might add, to answer the door. It was Matt. He was in sweatpants and a hoodie, and I must say, he looked handsome today. His face was unshaven, and his hair was messy.

"Good morning, Matt." I tried to sound cheery, although, admittedly, it was a strain. I was in pain, but not bad enough to warrant a trip to the ER.

"Just checking to see how you are doing this morning. Are you okay?"

"I've had better days, but I think I will live. Do you want to come in for a cup of coffee?"

"I could use one. Thanks." Matt followed me to the kitchen, but when I went to pour him a cup, he stopped me. "I can get it. You sit down. It doesn't look like you are moving around all that well right now. You look sore." I obeyed gladly and sat back down at the table, relieved to not have to reach for another mug, as getting mine was hard enough. I had no idea how I would get through the day at the bake-off, but I didn't feel like a had a choice because I didn't want to let Angela down.

"It still baffles me you weren't seriously injured in that wreck. Your car is a total write-off. I spoke with the towing company, and they said you can remove any of your personal items at their yard, once the insurance company has finished with the paperwork."

"Well, I must admit, I am pretty sore and slow moving this morning, but don't think it's anything time and rest won't heal. Unfortunately, I won't get any rest today because I have to be at the bake-off before nine this morning. But as soon as it is over, I am coming back here to veg for the next twenty-four hours, at least."

"Oh geeze, Sydney. Do you really have to go to the fair today? It's probably a good idea to lie low and rest after yesterday."

"I promised Angela that I would. She is away, and she has never missed a Main Street Business Bake-off Contest since owning Angela's Bookshop. So yes, I really have to go, unfortunately. Harry is loaning me his car and plans to meet up with me later." Although I didn't feel up to the contest today, I hoped that the distraction would help. And I knew how important this was. Even prior to Angela inheriting it from her father, he had also entered the bake-off with Angela's mom. At that time, the store name had simply been The Bookshop. But after Angela had done a complete makeover when her parents were gone, she decided a new updated store name would also be appropriate.

"I don't think you should go anywhere alone right now after what happened. Somebody wants to hurt you. And they already ran you off the road and destroyed your car. I'm not sure they're done with you yet, and that makes me very nervous. So, I have got someone keeping an eye on your house this morning. There is an officer parked outside on the street, and I will make sure he follows you to the fair. I will come by your bake-off booth to see you as soon as I finish up at the hospital. I got a call early this morning letting me know Eddie was conscious. The doctors said they would allow me to question him this morning. They just want to run some tests first."

I got up and shuffled slowly to peek through my front window. Sure enough, there was an officer sitting in his cruiser across the road from my house. When he saw me, he waved. I waved back. I sat back down and stared at Matt. "This is embarrassing. Now, everyone on my street will have seen him there, and be wondering what I have done wrong. I do not want him following me around the fairgrounds,"

"No, he won't follow you through the fairgrounds. I need him back at the station for the day because we are shorthanded right now. But I wanted to make sure you got there safe. At the fair, there should be enough people around to keep you safe." I mumbled in resistance. "This is for your safety. Someone tried to kill you yesterday, so

I'm sorry, Sydney, but this is not negotiable." I really didn't have the energy to argue with him right now, and I was well aware of the fact that someone tried to kill me yesterday. It was terrifying. I needed to find out who, before they attempted to hurt me again.

"I know I need the protection. But could you at least tell him to hang back a bit, so he doesn't make it so obvious that he is watching over me? Please?"

"I can do that. And if Eddie gives me any important information about the attempt on his life, I'll let you know. I suspect it is the same person who carried out the attacks on you, and they're likely related to Bob's death." Matt stood to leave. "See you later, Syd. I should be at the fair in a couple of hours."

As soon as Matt left, I went into high gear. It was almost eight, and I needed to leave in a couple of minutes. Gathering my stuff, I headed out to Harry's car, waving at the officer sitting in the cruiser again. Might as well be friendly. He was just doing his job. When I pulled out of the drive, the cop followed behind. I assumed Matt had already informed him of where I was going for the day. I would just try to focus on my task at hand. Bake a great French Apple Cake. Who knows? Maybe I could even bring a ribbon home for Angela's Bookshop.

Chapter 20

I flashed my pass at the gatekeepers of the fairgrounds, and they pointed out where I was to park, wishing me luck as I drove in. The parking area was already filling up with organizers and participants, but luckily, there was a spot reserved directly behind the arena for the bake-off contestants and inside vendors. Thankfully, the bake-off area was just inside the arena doors, so I didn't have far to walk. The fairgrounds were across from the arena parking area. Today, carnival rides, food trucks and face painting booths filled it. In the far back field, I could see dozens of horse trailers parked beside the two riding rings. From my vantage point, I couldn't make out any faces, but saw plenty of horses being led around by their riders. I made a mental note to go watch some of the horse events as soon as the bake-off competition was over. It had been a while since I had spent time around horses, and I missed it. When I was younger, I owned a beautiful bay gelding that I rode almost every day. I had him right until he died of old age. His intoxicating smell instantly entered my brain as I stood and watched. Maybe one day, I would get another horse. Gerard was never a fan and wasn't overly supportive of my riding, so when Benny passed, I didn't get another one. I think he might have been jealous of my love of all things horse related, and my horse riding friends too, which I couldn't understand because they were all so nice and we always tried to include him in things. Posh was also a horse lover and took riding lessons right until she left for university. I had no doubt she would return to riding horses one day. They were hard to quit.

I turned my attention back to the bake-off. The wide-open arena doors allowed me to walk straight through. Well, shuffle, not an actual walk, and it was at a snail's pace. The judge's table was just inside the doors to the left, with three chairs set up and waiting. Name tags marked each baking area, which had all the necessary equipment and ingredients for each contestant. There were only five entries, so the three double ovens in the kitchen behind us were enough for all the contestants. After promising Angela that I would take her place at the bake-off, I researched the history of the Blueberry Falls Fair and the annual bake-off competition. The first fall fair apparently occurred in 1881, and they constructed the arena in 1949. They built a new, upgraded kitchen in 1998. This coincided with the first annual Main Street Business Bake-off, an event that had become quite popular over the years. Angela said she hadn't missed a year since she took over the bookshop. I found the history of the village fascinating and had spent an entire afternoon looking up stuff online and even found a few old books about Blueberry Falls in her shop.

With a few minutes until the nine o'clock start, I surveyed the arena. There were dozens of tables, with different crafts and wares, all set up and ready to go for when the fair opened. Hopefully, after the contest was over, I would feel good enough to walk around and enjoy it all. My table was at the far end of the row of contestants. I was happy that Sandra Watt's table was right beside mine, so I at least knew one person in the contest. Sandra owned the antiques store next door to Sally's Café. Both our tables faced the parking lot. Next to Sandra was the owner of the Hair with Flare Salon. A pretty, lively young lady with an enthusiastic personality. She talked my ear off the first time I went in for a haircut. I couldn't remember her name. Jessie, or Josie, or Joanne, or some other J name, I think. Then there was the hardware store, and the pet store. Sally's Café hadn't entered the contest this year, but Angela had informed me she usually did.

Fifteen minutes before starting time, I saw Sandra rushing across the parking lot, looking flustered, so I met her halfway and relieved her of part of the armload of items she was carrying, despite the pain in my left arm still. "Oh, thank you, dear. I am so late! Had some car trouble this morning and it really put me behind. But I made it, so all's well that ends well, as they say." Sandra's hair flew out in all directions as she bustled to get set up. "How are you feeling today? You must be quite sore, I would imagine, but you don't look too worse for wear." She took her things from my arms and set them on her table. I winced.

"Not too bad." I lied.

She tilted her head, looking like she was going to disagree, but then took my word for it. Satisfied with her setup, she plopped herself heavily down in her chair and attempted to smooth out her flyaway hair. "My goodness, that was some morning, I tell ya."

"What happened?"

"I got my car all loaded and ready to go, then the darned thing wouldn't start. So, I had to take Harv's truck. Moved all my stuff over to his truck and rushed out the drive. Left him stranded with my silly, useless car. I'm betting he will have it up and running in no time at all, though. Him and Willy, that's my youngest son you met yesterday, seem to love working on vehicles. They can fix all sorts of things. Trucks. Tractors. Lawnmowers. You name it. My boys can do it all." Sandra barely stopped for a breath. "They said they'll be here later today. As soon as they get the car running again. Don't know what I'd do without them all. Oh, and Harv said to tell you he hopes you are doing okay after yesterday's fiasco." I don't know if I had ever known anyone that could talk as fast as Sandra.

Before she could continue, the judges came out and sat in their designated seats. The judges instructed us that the contest would begin in five minutes. Contestants would have two hours to complete their dish. "Here we go. Good luck Sandra." She smiled at me and hauled herself out of her chair, to stand ready to start at her table. I mentally reviewed my grandma's trusted French Apple Cake recipe in my head as I waited for the starting buzzer. I was ready for this.

Chapter 21

The next few hours flew by. I was happy with the results of my baking, and stood waiting, while the judges tested each of the five entries. Everything looked and smelled delicious. Eventually, I gave in and sat down to wait because I was getting pretty sore again. The baking occupied my mind, but the pain returned to the forefront now that I had stopped. I wasn't sure how much of the fair I could take in after the judges were done. Really, I just wanted to go home and rest now, but I also wanted to check things out and go see the horse show. To keep my mind from dwelling on my arm, I flipped through photos on my phone. I had forgotten to charge my phone last night and now my battery was almost dead. I also forgot to bring a phone charger. Ugh. One of my many bad habits. Regardless of battery life, I continued to scroll. After the bake-off, I planned to check Harry's car for a charger. I was sure I had seen one in there somewhere. I stopped on my photos of the big silver button from Eddie's barn floor. It had completely slipped my mind this morning to ask Matt about it. I wondered if he thought it was pertinent to the investigation. Or if any of the officers on the scene that day had even bothered to collect it from the barn floor for evidence after I had pointed it out to them, although I was sure they would have collected everything near where Eddie was lying. I would show Matt the photo as soon as he got here after talking to Eddie at the hospital. Or maybe I should send it to him right now so he can question Eddie about it while he is there, I thought. But before I could send it to him, the judges told us they were ready to announce a winner, so I slipped my phone into my back pocket, telling myself I would message him as soon as we finished.

It was a complete surprise when the judges announced my French Apple Cake as the runner-up. Second place. Not too shabby. I mean, I know I loved it and thought I had done a pretty good job of pulling off my grandma's favorite recipe today, but I was no chef. I walked up to collect my ribbon and felt my phone vibrating in my pocket. This was not the time to be pulling out a phone. Whoever it was, would have to wait until the bake-off was done. It was likely Harry telling me he was on his way to the fair with George. As I accepted the ribbon, I thought about my lovely grandma. She would have been so thrilled with all this. Trudy West, the co-owner of the hardware store, won the first prize, with her raspberry apple torte. Clapping her hands together in delight, Trudy ran up to claim her prize. The coveted trophy. They will engrave her business name on a plaque, mount it beside the past winners' plaques, so she could display it at her store until next year's contest, when they would pass it on to the next winner.

The moment the judges finished their announcements, I started packing my belongings. I figured I could throw it all in Harry's car, then have a look around the fair until Harry arrived with George. I was hurting, but could hang on a bit longer. After all, I had never been to a Blueberry Falls fair. In fact, it had been many years since I had been to any fair at all. It wasn't the kind of thing that interested Gerard, so we never went. "Sydney! Congratulations." Ellen was rushing across the arena towards my table, waving at me. "I hear you won second place with your cake. That's fantastic." News travels fast around here. As she congratulated me, she kept glancing over her shoulder, as if she expected someone to come up behind her. Lowering her voice, she whispered, "I'm heading home now." She again glanced over her shoulder. "Marty has been bugging me all morning. He just won't get the hint. And every time I turn around, I can feel him staring at me. I'm totally creeped out right now. I gave him the slip when I came in here. So, if you see him, please don't tell him you've seen me. She glanced over at Sandra, who was standing beside me, and Sandra nodded in agreement to keep quiet. Could you stop by on your way home when you're finished here? Keep me company for a bit. Nathan is going to stay at the hospital with his dad and then going to visit his girlfriend, so he won't be home. I just don't want to be alone right now. I don't feel safe with Marty stalking me today." Ellen's face was flushed from running through the crowd. Her eyes darted around, looking for signs of Marty. Something was really not right here. She was clearly in a panic.

"Don't you think maybe you should call the cops right now?" I suggested. "It sounds like he is taking this way too far." I felt like we should have been calling them immediately. This wasn't the first time Ellen had been upset and bothered by Marty, and he needed to be stopped from harassing her. Or stalking her. Or whatever it was they wanted to call it. Either way, it wasn't right.

"Yes, I will. As soon as I get home. But I just want to get out of here first. I will call them once I'm home. I am going to park my car in the garage, so Marty won't know I'm there. Hopefully, he will think I am somewhere on the fairgrounds still. When you're finished here, will you come by?" she pleaded.

"Of course I will. I was just going to have a wander around before I leave while I wait for Harry, then I'll be over. He should be here shortly. George is bringing him, because I had to take his car this morning."

"Oh? Why? Did yours break down?"

"Oh, you could say that. It's a long story. I will explain it all when I get to your place. You better get going, so you can give Marty the slip." Ellen nodded, then rushed out of the arena. Just as she was out of sight, I looked up to see Marty heading directly towards me. Wearing his ghastly jacket again. The jacket with the huge collar and big shiny silver buttons. He closed the gap fast with his long strides and was almost at my table. Suddenly, I gasped. "Oh, my Gawd." I mumbled. His jacket was missing a button. The button! "That's where I saw that button! I knew I had seen it before! Holy crap!" Sandra turned and looked at me in confusion.

"Did you say something to me?"

"Sorry Sandra. No, I didn't. Just talking to myself. I'll explain later. No time right now." Sandra had been listening to Ellen and me talking. Her eyes followed to where I was staring.

"Oh dear. It's Marty."

"Yup. It's Marty, and he's heading straight to us." Marty's strides were long, and he was covering ground fast. He had almost reached my table.

Marty strode directly to my table and put his long-fingered hands on the table so he could lean in further. "Have you seen Ellen?" He blurted out, looking around the arena instead of at me.

"Not today." I lied. Sandra clamped her mouth shut. "Marty, how are you? Are you enjoying the fair so far?" Marty merely grunted a quick reply, obviously not interested in any small talk with me. But I needed to delay him at the bake-off booth longer, so I tried again to get him chatting with me. "Would you like to try a piece of French Apple Cake? I won the second prize! Can you believe it?" I offered, hoping I could delay him long enough to allow Ellen to get out of the parking lot without Marty noticing her exit.

"No. I don't want cake," was all Marty said in response. He scanned the parking lot. Little beady eyes darting back and forth. I hadn't realized before just how creepy Marty made me feel. Ellen was right. He made me feel very uneasy. My chest tightened and my heart was beating fast. I was potentially standing in front of Eddie's attacker. So, of course I would feel panicked. Mostly for Ellen but even for Sandra and me as we stood in front of him lying to give Ellen more time to leave unnoticed. I couldn't believe I had forgotten where I had seen that silver button. If I had remembered, the police could have arrested him. Or at least had him on their radar. But now Ellen wasn't safe, and Marty was determined to find her. Marty had attacked Eddie. I was sure of it. I had no idea why, but I bet he also had something to do with Bob's death, too. And somehow, Ellen was his new target. But why?

I needed to call Matt, but couldn't do that while Marty was standing right in front of me within earshot. I had to make sure Matt could get over to Ellen's place right away. But I also needed to keep Marty busy here for a little while longer, so that he didn't see her leaving. If Ellen could get home and hide her car in the garage, she might be safe until I could get there with Harry and the police. Maybe then he would go back through the fairgrounds looking for her, and give Matt enough time to get to Ellen, or at least give me enough time to call Ellen and tell her Marty had come to my table looking for her already, and more importantly, to warn her I thought Marty was the one that attacked Eddie. I could feel my palms getting sweaty and my chest was thumping so loud, I felt sure others could hear it. Breathe, Syd, breathe. Just get him eating some cake and that will be enough time for Ellen to leave undetected. Sandra could keep feeding Marty while I called Matt. "What about some of Trudy's winning dessert, Marty? It's a delicious raspberry torte that she made. There's no wonder she won. It's out of this world delicious." I knew I was just rambling and wasting time. I just hoped it was enough to keep Marty's attention a bit longer.

"No, I don't want any dessert." He snapped at me. His tone was sharper now. I wasn't sure if he had somehow caught on to what I was up to. "I'm sure I saw her come this way. I wanted to talk to her about something. It's important. Are you sure you didn't see her?" Marty looked directly at me this time. Like he was trying to bore into my mind for information.

I tried my best to hold his stare as I answered. "Like I said. I haven't seen her. But if she comes by, I can tell her you're looking for her." I flashed Marty a big, fake smile. He didn't respond. He was no longer looking at me. I followed his gaze to the parking area. Ellen's little red car was just pulling out of the arena lot. Without another word, Marty went running out the arena doors. OMG! Marty had spotted Ellen. I watched as Marty rushed off towards the parking lot after Ellen. For a moment, I wasn't sure what I should do. If I called the police, it might be too late. Matt wasn't here to help. Harry hadn't arrived yet either. It was up to me to stop Marty. But how? I couldn't very well tackle him in the parking lot. Besides, he was well ahead of me now and I wasn't sure how fast I could even run today. Or any other day, for that matter. But I needed to do something. Anything other than just stand here, useless, watching Marty chase after my friend.

"Oh no! Sandra, I have to go right now! When Harry comes, tell him I am heading over to Ellen's place. And call the police. Please? I don't have time to call. I need to go after them and help Ellen! Oh, and tell them it was Marty that attacked Eddie and now Ellen is in grave danger."

Sandra's eyes went wide, and her mouth dropped open, but she nodded her head up and down. "Of course. Just help Ellen! I will tell them. Hurry! Ellen's safety is the priority." I didn't even pause to think the whole situation through. I just reacted with my gut. And my gut told me I needed to go after Marty and somehow stop him from getting to Ellen. I just hoped I could find a way to do that.

Sandra sprang into action right away. "I'll pack up your stuff and take it with me. Don't worry about anything, Sydney." She was already dialing the police before I left. "I'll call Matt too. You just go." She called out behind me, obviously sensing the urgency in the situation. "Be careful!" I heard her call out to me as I dashed across the parking lot towards Harry's car. I needed to get to Ellen before Marty did. It was surprising how fast I forgot about my injured arm while in panic mode to help Ellen. I sprinted across the parking lot to Harry's car as fast as I could.

Chapter 22

It's surprising how quickly I forgot about my injured arm in the midst of panic. The urgency of the situation pushed the pain to the back of my mind as I sprinted across the parking lot towards Harry's car. Initially, I thought of Marty as just a peculiar character. However, after hearing Ellen's concerns at the diner, I realized his fixation on her was excessive. It wasn't until now that I understood just how dangerous Marty could be. I now believed he was a dangerous stalker and possibly Bob's killer. As I ran, my eyes remained locked on Marty.

I could see Marty's bright-colored jacket well ahead of me in the distance. He was a lanky man, standing out above most of the vehicles. He was heading towards the far back corner of the lot, which would take some extra time. Harry's car was near the arena, but as I struggled to keep up, it seemed very far away. Huffing and panting pretty hard, I realized that joining the local gym, as Angela had suggested, might be a good idea once this was all over. Angela mentioned that many women my age went there and raved about their positive experiences with the trainers.

As I ran, I couldn't help but think about how my life had changed so drastically in such a short time. Just a few weeks ago, my focus was on my work and coffee mornings with Harry. Now, I was chasing a potential killer through a parking lot, my heart pounding with fear and adrenaline. The realization that Marty might be Bob's killer sent chills down my spine. I felt a mix of anger and determination. I had to protect Ellen, no matter what.

By the time I reached Harry's car, my breath came in ragged gasps. I glanced over to where Marty had gone and saw him getting into a black truck—the same truck with the menacing front grill that had run me off the road. My stomach churned with fear. Fumbling in my jacket pocket for the keys, my fingers finally found them. I hurriedly tried to stick the key into the lock, but I couldn't get my hands to work properly because they shook so much. My clumsiness frustrated me, and my mom's words echoed in my mind, "More hurry, less speed, Syd." It was true. I took a deep breath. Mum's words were a reminder to stay calm and focused, even in the most chaotic situations. I knew I had to keep my wits about me if I was going to help Ellen.

I quickly slid into the driver's seat, just as Marty's truck pulled out of its spot and headed towards the exit. Relief washed over me when he didn't look in my direction. Keeping a safe distance, I dialed Ellen's number, my fingers trembling. The phone rang, but there was no answer. "Oh, shoot!" I muttered, trying her number again. Still no answer. Panic surged through me. There were two vehicles between Marty and me, and I knew from watching cop shows he would notice if I followed too closely. I had to be inconspicuous.

My mind raced. What would I do once I got to Ellen's place? Tackling Marty to the ground was out of the question. I needed help. I hoped Sandra had reached the police and that they were taking her call seriously. But what if they didn't? The uncertainty gnawed at me.

I tried calling Ellen one more time. If I could warn her that Marty was close behind, maybe I could convince her to drive to the police station instead of hiding out at home. I felt the situation was much more dire than she realized. There was no answer still. I reached across the seat and popped the glove box open, hoping Harry's charger was inside. Nope. My low battery warning flashed across my screen. Crap! Next, I tried calling Matt. Frantic to get a hold of somebody before my phone died. Too late. Before the call went through, my screen went black. Totally dead. Just my luck with timing. Frustrated, I threw the phone onto the seat beside me. Why didn't I bring my charger? Or charge it last night at least? I knew why. Last night, I had been exhausted and in a lot of pain. Never mind being extremely upset over the entire ordeal of being run off the road and totaling my car. Also, this morning I had been in such a rush to get to the fair and was pre-occupied with managing my pain while carrying everything I needed for the bake-off.

Still following behind at a distance, my mind wandered once again to the missing button on Marty's jacket and the button I had seen on the floor of Eddie's barn. I thought about Eddie laying on the barn floor. What would have happened to him if we hadn't come by right then? I suspected we may have had another dead body. I realized now that Eddie was trying to tell me about Marty and to warn Ellen too, but I hadn't understood his utterings. Although I knew Ellen was in danger, the reason remained unclear. What did Bob, Ellen, Eddie and Marty have in common? I just couldn't figure it out. And what was Marty's motive? All I really knew about him so far was that he had a very serious crush, no, scratch that, an obsession with Ellen. I still didn't know if Marty had anything to do with Bob's death. Or if it was one of the other suspects Harry and I had listed. I strongly doubted Sandra had anything to do with it. She didn't have a motive that I knew of, and besides, she had an alibi. George was a bit of a troublemaker with all of his gossip, but he also had an alibi, and no real motive. Nathan Caldwell was still on the list. He seemed quite protective of his mother, and maybe he had some of his father's anger issues. I saw him and Ellen arguing the other day in the park. But with

Eddie's attack, I had ruled Nathan out in my mind. Nathan and his dad were close, according to Ellen.

A delivery truck pulled out right in front of me, pulling me out of my thoughts, as I hit the brakes to avoid running into the back of it. Now I had lost sight of Marty's truck. My guess was that he was following Ellen, so all I could do was continue heading to her place, or hope the truck turned off somewhere, so I could continue tracking Marty. No such luck. The truck came to a complete stop in front of me and threw on their four-way flashers. "Are you kidding me!? You stop right in the middle of the road and block all the traffic?" I muttered to myself. I looked around and saw that the driver couldn't pull over because parked cars lined the entire curb. There really weren't that many places to park in downtown Blueberry Falls. I couldn't go around because there was a steady stream of traffic passing by the other way, so I would have to wait, losing precious time in my precarious situation. Despite my desperation, I realized the delivery driver was unaware of my need to get by him. I cursed myself again for not keeping my phone charged. It was a bad habit that I needed to break, for sure. I watched as the driver ran into a store with a parcel and moments later, ran back out and jumped back into the truck. I was relieved at his quick drop off. How was he to know I was on the heels of a likely killer and trying to save my friend's life? I prepared to pull out once the truck got moving, but the driver jumped back out with another parcel and headed down the street to the next building, where he disappeared inside the door of the hardware store. I threw Harry's vehicle back into park with a huff and banged on the steering wheel.

Although Blueberry Falls was a quaint town, known for its charming streets lined with historic buildings and cozy cafes, sometimes it got pretty busy. The downtown area was always bustling with activity, especially on weekends when locals and tourists alike flocked to the farmers' market and various shops. The narrow streets and limited parking spaces often made navigating through the town a challenge, however, that usually added to the town's unique charm. Today was different because of the fall fair, which brought in more people than usual. The streets were a flurry of activity. I realized the delivery truck driver could not have known anything about my situation and the fact that I had to catch up to Marty and Ellen but he seemed oblivious to the chaos he was causing, as he took his time with the delivery and I was starting to panic. Each second ticked by in slow motion as I anxiously waited for him to get moving again. My heart pounded in my chest, and I could feel the sweat forming on my forehead. The urgency of the situation was overwhelming, and I couldn't help but feel frustrated at the delay. Finally, after what felt like an eternity, the driver returned to his truck and we were moving again. He turned off at the next corner, and I sped up to catch up to Marty, but his truck was nowhere in sight.

Chapter 23

Ellen's house was only three down from the corner, so it was in sight as soon as I turned onto her street. The street was empty of vehicles. I pulled in front of a house across the road from her neighbors and parked. It was close enough to give me a clear, unobstructed view, while hopefully not catching Marty's attention. Ellen's house had character and stood out among the others on the street with its charming appearance. A neatly trimmed hedge bordering the property by the road showed meticulous maintenance of the front yard. The house itself had wood siding that was painted a soft shade of blue, with lovely white shutters and an oversized covered front porch. Potted plants and white railings adorned the porch. At the one end, there was a cozy swing big enough for two people.

The entire neighborhood was quiet and peaceful. The chirping of birds and the gentle rustling of leaves created a false sense of sereneness. All things I hadn't noticed when I was here before, which seemed so strange to me. Why was I noticing these details now? As I took in the entire scene, I realized everything looked so picturesque. It was a stark contrast to the actual tension and danger of the moment. My eyes darted back and forth as I attempted to form a plan in my mind to help Ellen. I could see Marty's black pickup parked in Ellen's driveway. He had pulled his truck right up to the garage door. The garage door was wide open. And Marty's truck completely blocked Ellen's car inside. Obviously, Ellen hadn't arrived in time to hide her car before Marty got there. This wasn't good at all.

I saw movement in the garage, so I slid down low in the seat to stay out of sight. Hopefully, Marty hadn't noticed me. I was in Harry's car, so it was unlikely that he would think it was me, anyway. Marty and Ellen walked towards the front door. He had hold of her arm, steering Ellen along the path. As they walked past the garbage cans set along the wall, Marty stopped and pulled something out from the top of the can. I couldn't quite tell what it was at first, but then realized it was the flowers from Marty that Ellen had said she would throw away. He started waving them at her, and Ellen's frame shrunk back, cowering away from Marty. When they got to the front door, he shoved her inside, turned to look around the street, then went inside, shutting the door behind them. I watched from my seat. I had no idea what I was supposed to do next. Unable to contact anyone because of my dead cell phone, I knew I couldn't simply wait for the police without taking action. Ellen was in danger, and every part of me screamed to help her. I could see them both as they moved into the living room. Marty steered Ellen over to the couch and pushed her down. I was too far away to see Ellen's face clearly, but knew she must have been terrified. Oh, my dear friend. *I'm here Ellen. I'm coming to help*, was what I wanted to tell her. But all I did was sit and watch. Marty stood over her, waving the flowers back and forth in front of him. He appeared to be yelling something, and I could only assume it had something to do with the flowers. Just a wild guess, since he still waved the bouquet back and forth in aggressive motions. Then Marty suddenly stopped and walked towards the front window. He looked in both directions along the street, likely checking if anyone had witnessed anything so far. I once again slipped down low in the seat, hoping he hadn't seen me. After a few minutes, I took a chance and lifted my head up just enough so I could peek out the car window. Marty had pulled the drapes closed, and I could no longer see inside.

This was my chance to exit the car and get across the road without him seeing me. But where could I hide out of sight once I left the vehicle? There was a red truck parked in the neighbor's driveway, which was right beside Ellen's driveway, divided only by a thin strip of grass, not even as wide as a lawnmower. Kind of silly to have it there, but I suppose it made a proper division of the two properties. Each house was a mirror of the other. However, the difference in how much attention and care they received was obvious, making the houses look very different. I noticed the subtle details that made Ellen's house unique - the vintage lanterns hanging on either side of her garage doors. The neighboring garage had none. And Ellen had a lovely flower garden on her front lawn, with whimsical little garden gnomes peeking out from behind groupings of flowers. Next door was absent of any flower gardens. Instead, it had an unkempt hedge along the front of the property, and an overgrown lawn. Each house had a single garage. Ellen's garage had a walkway of patio stones running along the side of it. The neighbor's was a dirt path.

The red truck was directly across the road from where I had pulled up, and I doubted Marty could see me from there. I just needed to get across the road unnoticed. I opened my door and readied myself to run, but quickly shut it again when I heard a commotion coming from the road behind me. In my rearview mirror, I saw a small group of teens walking up the middle of the road towards Harry's parked car. To be fair, I must say, there wasn't a sidewalk for them to use and there was no traffic on the road. There were five of them. They were all laughing and chatting. So animated. So happy. They reminded me of Posh with her friends and I felt a pang of sadness as I thought about how much I missed her some days. Even though she was only a phone call away, it wasn't the same as having her close by. Her apartment in Ottawa was almost five hours' drive, and she was busy with her new job, so I didn't see her nearly as often as I would have liked. I waited until the group had passed and was almost out of sight, then I stepped out of the car and darted across the road and ducked behind the red truck. I was determined not to let anything happen to Ellen, but had no idea how I was going to pull that off.

As I crouched behind the truck, I tried to figure out how to get inside undetected. Now that the teen group was out of sight, I saw no other people. No one was coming to help me rescue Ellen. I was on my own in this. All I could hope for at this point was that Sandra had succeeded in contacting the police and Matt. And possibly even Harry and George by now. I had to get from the truck to the side of Ellen's house while Marty still had the curtains drawn shut, so I took the chance and ran the short distance, stopping to lean on the outside wall of the garage. Beside me was the gate to Ellen's backyard, where I remembered there was a back door off the kitchen. My heart pounded in my chest as I crept through the shadows of the backyard. The plan was to sneak in through the back door and somehow talk Marty into leaving peacefully. I tried to calm my escalating panic. Despite the chill in the air today, sweat beaded on my forehead and my hands were clammy. When I reached the back door, I carefully turned the handle, praying it wouldn't creak, but my grip slipped from all the sweat, so I wiped my hands on my pants and tried again. I turned the handle ever so slowly, not daring to make any noise.

Chapter 24

Luckily, the door was unlocked, so I cracked it open to peek inside. I couldn't see them. The swinging door to the living room was closed, thankfully. Ellen's little dog was yapping frantically from the other room. His noise, at least, was beneficial as I attempted to remain quiet. I pushed gently on the door, and it swung open silently, and I slipped inside.

"Shut that dog up or I will," Marty threatened.

"Marty, sh…she's just sc..sc,,scared." Ellen stuttered. "She's barking because she's locked in her crate and can't get to me. She will calm down in a minute. I'm sure she will." Ellen pleaded with Marty. "Ppp…please don't hu..hurt her." Ellen was sobbing now. "Maybe if you sit down and stop yelling at me, she will be quiet, too." Ellen's voice trembled as she attempted to reason with Marty, unsuccessfully. I nudged the swinging door just enough to allow me to see them both through the crack.

"I'm not yelling." Marty's gruff voice lowered a few decibels. "I'm sorry. Ellen, please don't be scared. I really don't want to scare you. I just want to be with you, so you know how much I care." Marty's voice softened, just for a moment, before snapping again. "You need to make your dog be quiet. It's making me angry Ellen. And I don't want to be angry with you."

Ellen sat forward on the couch and pointed her finger at the dog. "Quiet, Stella," she instructed her dog, who, surprisingly, listened to her, stopped the loud barking and lay down in the crate.

"Why did you throw my flowers out, Ellen? I sent you gifts, and you refused them." Marty's voice was loud again as he waved the flowers at Ellen, then threw them on the floor in disgust.

"I'm sorry. I shouldn't have done that. Really Marty. Can't we just talk about this without you yelling at me? You said you didn't want to scare me, but you are! You are really scaring me." I could hear the confidence and assertiveness returning to Ellen's voice, and it gave me hope as I listened to her trying to reason with Marty. "Why don't I make us a coffee and we can sit and talk about it all?" Ellen pleaded with Marty, which was brilliant. I glanced around the room looking for something to arm myself with in case they came into the kitchen for coffee and grabbed a cast iron fry pan hanging above the stove. It was heavy. This ought to do. I could strike him in the head when he came through the door. It always worked in the movies, so it seemed reasonable to me it would work in this situation.

"I don't want to sit, and I don't want coffee." Marty snapped at Ellen as he threw the flower bouquet at her. Instead of hitting her with them, they landed on the arm of the couch beside her. "Why did you put up with Eddie and Bob, but you wouldn't even have dinner with me? I asked you twice, and you made up some lame excuse for not going. Why couldn't you give me a chance? Get to know me. I'm a good person. But you have made me resort to this!" Marty waved his arms around the room. "You made me do this. I wouldn't have had to follow you here and make you talk to me if you had just given me a chance. This is your fault. Not mine." While Marty's reasoning was completely out of whack, he appeared to genuinely believe it. "I didn't mean to scare you Ellen, but I love you and I know that once you get to know me better, you will learn to love me too. I would never treat you like that wicked ex-husband of yours did. Or like that cheater, Bob. You deserve better. You deserve someone like me. We will be perfect together, and you will never have to worry about Eddie or Bob again."

The whole time that Marty was explaining why he was holding her captive, Ellen's head just kept swinging back and forth slowly. "Oh, no Marty! No, no, no," Ellen repeated over and over while her head kept swinging. Her eyes bulged and were now locked directly on Marty as he paced back and forth across the living room in front of her. "What have you done Marty? Were you the one the hurt Eddie? And Bob too!? Did you kill Bob?" The words screeched out as Ellen took in what Marty was saying to her. I could hear the panic in her voice and knew I had to act soon. I continued to watch and listen quietly, peeking through the door to the living room. Ellen still sat on the couch. Her head was swinging side to side as tears streamed down her face.

"They both deserved it," Marty snapped back. "Bob was a lying, no good cheater. He got what was coming to him. He dumped you like a piece of garbage to go back to his wife. Ellen, he never loved you. But I love you. I would never treat you like that. I won't ever cheat on you or leave you."

OMG Marty killed Bob! I had been positive that Marty had attacked Eddie after seeing the missing button on his jacket, but until now, I hadn't been sure about his role in Bob's death. Marty was certifiably crazy!! I watched helplessly as my friend's mouth dropped open in utter shock.

"And that no-good ex-husband of yours was a drunk that gambled all his money away. He thought he could just threaten anyone that ever stood up to him. I tried to tell him he didn't deserve you. But all he did was get mad. Then he attacked me. He beat me up, and I ended up in the hospital. I knew he would do that because he was always losing his cool at the bar. All it took was someone to argue with him and call him a name, and he would start swinging. He had no control. It was so easy. I planned to come back to Blueberry Falls after Eddie was out of the way. I knew I would be your hero when I saved you. And now my plan is almost complete. You will see."

Wait! What?! I tried to comprehend what Marty had just said. What was he talking about? When did Eddie attack him? I couldn't piece it all together. Something still didn't make sense. I thought Marty was new to Blueberry Falls.

"YOU!" Ellen spat at Marty. "I never saw you because I didn't go to the trial, but I remember the name of the guy that made sure Eddie got locked up. James Martin Williams. That's you. Oh, my Gawd." Marty smiled. A slow, wicked smile that spread across his entire face. A Cheshire cat.

"You were the reason Eddie went to jail, weren't you? I know he shouldn't have hit you. He shouldn't have been drinking, and he shouldn't have been fighting. But everyone that saw the fight that night said you purposely goaded him into hitting you. Eddie's Uncle Gus said he overheard you at the courthouse. You were telling someone that you had been wanting Eddie out of the way for a long time. It made little sense back then. But it makes sense now. That was your plan all along, wasn't it?" I watched and listened as Ellen put the pieces together. Now it made more sense. Marty must have been stalking Ellen for a long time. I don't know when or where he first put his plan into action, but it was at least a couple of years ago.

"You bet I had a plan. A good one too, because it worked. Eddie went to jail and that meant he was out of the way so I could come in and save you. Ever since that very first time we met, when you served me at the cafe, I knew I had to marry you. I knew then that we would be together. Don't you remember?"

Ellen's brows wrinkled as she tried to remember. "I saw so many people every day when I was working at the cafe. I couldn't possibly remember everyone that I served."

"You only had eyes for your stupid drunk husband. I could see that. And I could see that he didn't deserve you. I knew I had to do something so that one day you would be mine. All mine. I had to get Eddie out of your life. And it was working. I was so close. But I had to wait. I had to give you time after he got locked up. And then I was going to move to Blueberry Falls and sweep you off your feet. We were finally going to be together. It was all working out perfect." Marty paused for a moment before continuing. "But when I got here, you were already with that cheater,

Bob. So I went to see Bob at the bowling alley. I told him I was going to tell his wife all about the affair if he didn't break it off with you. And that would have worked fine. But Bob lied and said he already broke it off with you. He said his wife already knew. And he got mad. Real mad. He said he was going to tell the police about me. Then he said I was trespassing and had to leave and never come back. So when he turned around, I pushed him. I didn't mean to kill him. But he deserved it. He was a cheater. And he didn't deserve you."

As I peeked through the door, I noticed Marty had stopped pacing. He was just standing and looking at Ellen. "We are going to go away, and you are going to learn to love me. Just wait and see Ellen. I have the most beautiful cabin all ready for us. I am taking you there today."

"No, I won't go with you. I'm not going anywhere with you, and I will never love you."

"Oh yes you are, and you are going to write your boy a nice letter, so he knows you are okay, and doesn't go do something stupid like call the cops on us."

"I won't go with you, and I could never love you!" Ellen screamed at Marty defiantly. "You killed Bob and I hate you. I will always hate you. You are a monster." Ellen's screaming turned to sobbing as she buried her face in her hands. The realization that Bob was dead because of Marty was simply too much.

"Yes, you are Ellen. You are coming with me. You don't have a choice right now," Marty said confidently. He had his back to me now. This was my chance. Maybe my only chance. I took a deep breath, then shoved the door as hard as I could, knocking Marty forward a couple of steps. Springing into the room, I swung the frying pan as hard as I could right at Marty's head, but he moved too quickly, and the pan only caught his left shoulder. It hit with a loud thud, and Marty screamed out in pain. He spun around fast, and his eyes blazed with fury. His left fist connected with my cheek, sending me flying to the floor. I was about to get up and try again, but stopped in my tracks. I froze, still on the ground, with Marty towering over me. He had a gun pointed directly at me. I had no idea where it came from. He must have had it tucked in his belt or something.

"Get up." Marty commanded as he waved the gun at me. "That was a stupid move, Sydney. I mean, really, stupid. And now I am mad. You should have minded your own business. I tried to warn you away, but you ignored my note. And you didn't even take being run off the road as a hint. Now, here you are, and I am going to have to do something about you before I take Ellen with me." I got up and stood by the swinging kitchen door. I could barely breathe, and I could hear my heart pounding in my ears.

Panic was setting in fast. I needed to stay calm and think. It was the only way I was going to find a way out of this extremely bad predicament. Now, instead of just Ellen being in danger, we both were. I had no doubt that Marty would shoot me. After all, he had already killed Bob and attempted to kill Eddie, too. Who knew how many others Marty had harmed before?

"You're right, Marty. I'm sorry. I shouldn't have come here. But you don't have to hurt me. Or Ellen. We will co-operate. I will do whatever you ask. Just don't hurt us." I knew I had to stay calm and keep talking to him. I needed Marty to keep calm, too, and I needed the police to hurry and get here. This situation was beyond my capabilities. Marty believed that murdering Bob and attacking Eddie were justifiable, so it wasn't too farfetched to think he could also justify killing me in his mind. I had messed up with the frying pan. If I hadn't missed his head, I might have knocked him out so Ellen and I could escape. But now, I had a gun waving in my face. I was scared. Think Sydney, think! Inhaling and exhaling deeply, I faced Marty and his gun. The look on his face was terrifying. He was beat red. Even his eyes were red. Horns could have grown from his head, and it wouldn't have surprised me. I looked around the room without moving my head too much. I needed to find something I could throw at him or hit him with again. Hopefully, with greater success than my first attempt. On the side table beside the couch were the two marble dice that Eddie and Ellen had brought back from India. One time, when I came to visit Ellen, she saw me admiring them and had told me they were from their honeymoon trip many years ago. On the other side table was a large glass bowl, but that was out of reach. Other than that, and the lamp in the corner, I saw nothing else that might have been helpful.

"Not for one minute do I believe you will suddenly start cooperating with me, Sydney. I'm not stupid. I don't trust you at all. Now you have forced my hand, and I will have to kill you." I gasped as I tried to gulp air. My ears were ringing so loud, I couldn't hear anything else. I shook my head fiercely back and forth.

"No Marty. You don't have to do that." Before I could say anything more, Marty cut me off.

"Shut up! This is all your fault. So don't start begging me now. I warned you. You refused to listen!" Marty's face looked contorted. His beady eyes appeared to bulge right out of his head. "Stop standing there like some idiot. Go sit on the couch beside Ellen. Now!" His voice rose an entire octave. He was losing control, and I had just made it worse. I needed to figure something out. And fast! As I took a tentative step towards the couch, Marty shoved me forward. "Faster. Stop playing games." This was my chance, I thought. I pretended to lose my balance and fell forward towards the table beside the couch. Reaching my arms out to stop my fall, I grabbed the smaller marble die in my hand. It was heavier than I thought it would be, but that was good. As I straightened up, I dropped it into my sweater pocket, hoping that Marty hadn't noticed. Then I took a seat next to Ellen, who sat shaking on the couch.

"Don't worry Ellen. We are going to be okay." I said, even though I wasn't convinced we would be at this point. I reached out and patted her leg, hoping to comfort her slightly.

"Keep your hands to yourself and don't say another word" I drew my hand back to my side, feeling the heavy marble weapon in my pocket. It was a slight comfort in this horrible situation.

Chapter 25

Ellen's sparsely decorated living room housed the large leather couch that Ellen and I sat on, a recliner in the corner of the room, with a lamp behind it, and an over-filled bookcase beside it. It was a cozy looking reading corner, with a soft white throw blanket draped over the chair, and a pillow with cartoon dogs all over it. Marty paced back and forth in the middle of the room, muttering to himself, and occasionally at us. I couldn't make out what he was muttering about, but he certainly appeared to be disturbed. Finally, he turned and faced directly at me, waving his gun at me. The way he was handling the gun terrified me. It could easily go off accidentally. His face was still all red and blotchy. I almost wondered if he was going to have a heart attack or something. I could only hope. Sweat beaded on his forehead. "I don't have a choice. You interfered and tried to wreck my plan, but you won't stop us. We are going to have a great life together. You will not ruin that for us." Holy cow, he had gone right off the deep end. Although I believed he was beyond reason at this point, I knew I still had to try.

"Now I am forced to kill you. You stupid lady. You have left me no choice. Why did you have to ruin it for us? If you had just minded your own business, you wouldn't be in this mess right now." Ellen was shaking so much, I could feel it through the couch. I wanted to comfort her, but I didn't want to get Marty mad again. And I most definitely did not want to get shot. He was clearly unstable, and anything could set him off.

I have to get us out of this somehow. I looked around the room. In the far corner, Ellen's little dog Stella lay quietly in her crate. Thank Gawd for that. I think Marty might have shot the dog if she had continued yapping at him. But the poor thing looked scared as she lay there, resting her head on her front paws, and her eyes following Marty's every move. I knew I had to get us out of here, but how? Marty had a gun and was willing to use it. We sat so close that I doubted he would miss. I did not want to die. If I couldn't reason with him, maybe I could at least buy us some time. At least delay things until the police arrived. I wondered if Sandra was successful in convincing them that this was a dire situation. Were they even coming to help us? It seemed like I had been here long enough that they should have been here by now, but I couldn't hear any sirens coming to our rescue.

"Why did you kill Bob?" Maybe I could get him talking and somehow distract him.

"Why should I explain it to you?"

"So that I can understand. You said you love Ellen, but did you really have to kill Bob?"

"I already told Ellen it was an accident. Killing him was unintentional. I pushed him because he made me mad. Then he fell and hit his head."

"Okay, so it was an accident. Sometimes dreadful accidents happen. But I don't think you are a bad guy, Marty. And maybe we could explain it to the police. You can tell them how sorry you are that Bob died. That it was an argument that went wrong. I bet they would be lenient with you. What do you say?"

"I'm not sorry Bob's dead. And I'm not giving myself up. Bob was a no-good, lying cheater. And he should have stayed away from Ellen. He ruined my plan. Bob already had a wife. But he was greedy, and he deserved to die. He never cared about my Ellen. He never loved her. I could tell he didn't love her like I love her. Bob didn't deserve someone like Ellen. But I do. And I am going to treat her so good. We will be so happy." Then he turned to Ellen. "You will see, my love. Just you wait and see." His face softened for a moment as he talked to Ellen. Then Marty turned back to me and growled in a low, barely audible voice. "If you think I am going to turn myself in, then you are crazy. I am leaving with Ellen. So shut up.

Because you are making me mad and then I'm going to just shoot you right there on the couch." I did not question that his threat was real. He had already threatened to kill me. But I had to keep trying.

"If you just tie me up instead of shooting me, you can still escape. You don't need to kill me, Marty." My plea fell on deaf ears.

"Don't say another word. I mean it!" Marty pointed the gun directly at me. As I shrunk back on the couch, I slipped my hand into my pocket and wrapped my fingers tightly around the heavy marble die. My plan was to throw it as hard as I could at Marty and hope to at least knock him off balance long enough for one of us to escape and get help.

I knew I would only have one chance, so I had to make it a good one. The marble weapon was heavy, which was good. Hopefully, heavy enough. It had to work. I used to have a good aim. And I could throw hard too. But it had been almost ten years since I had played on the lady's softball team. I had tossed a ball around a few times since then, but not enough to feel confident I could hit my target with one shot. *You got this, Syd. This is your only chance, so just don't miss. Do not mess this up!*

With Marty focused on Ellen, I quickly pulled my hand from my pocket, sat forward on the couch, and hurled the heavy marble die directly at his head with all my might. It hit the side of Marty's head with a loud crack and sent him staggering sideways. Blood appeared instantly as the corner of the cube had cut into his head. He dropped his gun, and I immediately jumped up off the couch, lunging at him with my whole body and tackling him to the ground. "Run Ellen! Run! Now!" Before I could say more, I felt a sharp pain in my ear as Marty punched me.

We rolled back and forth across the carpet as we wrestled. I could not hold him much longer. He was stronger than me. And agile. All I could see were Ellen's feet as she ran towards the front door to escape. She reached the door and began screaming for help as soon as she pulled it open. Thank Gawd. She's safe, I thought, but the relief didn't last because I then saw that Marty's outstretched hand could almost reach his gun only a few feet away. *He cannot get to that gun! Stop him, Syd!* I urged myself to try harder. To be stronger. Or I was going to lose the fight. And then, somehow, from somewhere deep inside, I pulled some reserve strength. Using my upper body, I covered Marty's head and pulled his outstretched arm back from the gun. I was slowing him down, but it wasn't enough. He was too strong for me. Marty swung at me again and I ducked my head to the side. As I did, I spotted the lamp cord and pulled it off the table, towards me. The lamp landed on the carpet within reach, so I picked it up and smashed it into the back of Marty's head, just as his fingers reached the gun. His head fell forward onto the carpet. As I struggled to get up and away from him, Matt burst through the front door, gun drawn and pointed at Marty, with three more officers following right behind. By this time, I was still struggling. My whole body was quickly turning to Jello. I had only made it to a kneeling position, but was struggling hard to stand up. I had used everything I had to fight Marty. There was nothing left. Matt kicked the gun away from Marty's limp hand and turned to help me up. He had to lift me to my feet and hold, while I fought to steady myself.

"Are you okay?" I said nothing and just crumpled into Matt's arms as relief washed over me. He held me tight for a moment. I was alive. Only a few seconds ago, I truly thought I was going to die. I fought the tears that threatened and shakily stepped away from Matt's comforting embrace.

"Yes, I'm okay," as I attempted to stand straight. I winced. A sharp pain shot down my back and leg. Matt's arm shot out to support me. "Well, maybe not as okay as I thought." I admitted. "But I'm alive, and up to a couple of minutes ago, I didn't think I was going to get us away from Marty. I thought he was going to kill me. He is totally crazy, Matt. I mean, off the charts."

"Let's get you out to the ambulance so the paramedics can take care of you and get you to the hospital.

You can give me all the details there once I am finished up here. Can you walk, or do you need them to come in with the stretcher?"

"I think I would rather walk, but might need a bit of help." Matt practically carried me out to the waiting paramedics. As they loaded me into the ambulance, I saw Marty being escorted out in handcuffs. He had regained consciousness, and was glaring at me with his awful, beady eyes. Blood still dripped down the side of his head from where the marble die had made contact. That wonderful little object had helped save both Ellen and me. A shiver ran through me, and I looked away from his awful glare as the ambulance doors closed.

Chapter 26

"Even though I don't have any broken bones or anything, they told me I needed to stay overnight just to be safe." I explained. "The doctor said there was a lot of bruising and swelling and he wanted to run more tests tomorrow. Just in case there is internal bleeding or something." Harry nodded from the chair beside my hospital bed as he held my hand.

"I don't know how you fought him off Syd. Marty's not a small guy. He's got to be over six feet. When Sandra told me you had gone chasing after him, I near lost my mind. If anything had happened to you, I would never forgive myself. I mean, it was me who asked you to help find Bob's killer, and it's my fault you put yourself in danger today. He could have killed you, Sydney. You should have waited for someone before you went inside to confront that monster. Promise me you won't do anything that crazy again, please." I had never seen Harry so upset. He patted my hand gently and searched my eyes for some sort of agreement.

"Harry, this was not your fault! I went after Marty. That was all me. Not you. And you didn't make me help you. I said I would help you because I wanted to. I love a good mystery. Solving puzzles has always been something I was good at. This wasn't the first time I've found myself in a predicament because of my nosey investigations, and it likely won't be my last. But I never want to have a gun pointed at me again. That was terrifying. And I promise to lie low and mind my own business, at least for the next little while." Harry laughed.

"You are one tough lady, Sydney Jones." He stood and grabbed his jacket off the back of the chair. "I am going to go visit Victoria now. She called earlier asking if I would come sit with her for a while. The police had just left after informing her of Marty's arrest and she's quite upset about the whole thing. I don't blame her. Once this all gets out, the town is going to be buzzing with all sorts of gossip. I will be back here tomorrow to bring you home, okay?"

"Thanks Harry. For everything." Harry stood in the doorway. "Thanks for being the best next-door neighbor I've ever had. And for being such a great friend. Oh, and also, for all our morning coffee chats. I don't know what I would have done without you over the last few months. You were my first new friend here, and I really lucked out."

"Now you are just getting sappy, girl. Get some rest. I'll see you tomorrow once you get the all clear to go."

He blew me a kiss as he walked out the door, which made me laugh. I closed my eyes for a moment to rest. A few minutes later, a nurse came in and gave me something for the pain. Well, this should help, I thought, as I dozed off. I don't know how long I slept, but a dream of being shot jolted me awake with a scream.

"Hey Sydney. You're okay. Just a bad dream." As my eyes focused, I saw Matt standing over me, brows all wrinkled. I was so confused. "You're at the hospital. You're safe now. Marty is being held for court and, with the evidence we have on him now, it's unlikely he will be free for a very long time."

Slowly, the events of the day came back. I struggled to sit up but was so sore, I could barely move. "Wait. Let me help you. I will put your bed up instead." Matt cranked the bed to a sitting position. It felt better. I rested my head back on my pillow and sipped on the water he had just handed me.

"I'm good now. Thanks. I don't know what those meds were that they gave me, but they knocked me right out. I woke up all confused, but I'm okay now. Just a little sore is all. The doctor says I'll be good to go home tomorrow. Nothing major. Where's Ellen? Is she okay?"

"She is doing well. Because of you, she was unharmed. She's waiting out in the hall to see you." Matt sat down on the side of my bed. He stayed silent for a couple of minutes, looking like he wanted to say something. Finally, he asked. "Why didn't you call me back when you got my message about what Eddie had told me about Marty? And why didn't you call me before chasing after the guy who had attacked Eddie? I mean, I explained to you how dangerous Marty was, but you confronted him anyway." Matt's brow wrinkled as he kept his eyes locked on mine. I didn't hear anger in his voice like I would have expected from him. Maybe frustration? I could only assume that he was trying hard not to get too mad at me since I was injured and lying in a hospital bed.

"Matt, I didn't get any message from you. I was at the bake-off all morning, then Ellen came by and told me she was going home because Marty's behavior was making her nervous. I told Ellen I would go see her as soon as I was done." As I explained, I remembered my phone buzzing in my pocket that I had ignored during the contest. It must have been Matt. "I must have missed you call during the bake-off. And almost immediately after Ellen left the fair, Marty came over to my table looking for her. He caught sight of Ellen as she was leaving and went running after her. I knew I had to help Ellen, so I asked Sandra to call 911 and you. I didn't want to waste any time, so I followed Marty. Ellen needed to know Marty was right behind her. I tried to call her and tell her to drive straight to the police station instead of her house, but she didn't answer her phone." Matt moved his head up and down slowly as he took in my explanation.

"Okay, I get that Sydney. But why didn't you call me before you got to Ellen's place? Or at least before you went inside and put your life in danger? He could easily have killed you."

"Everything happened so fast. And I tried to call you, but my phone died while I was following Marty and Ellen. I couldn't pick up your message and I couldn't call anyone for help. All I could do was hope that Sandra had succeeded in contacting you."

"We got a 911 call from Sandra. And when it came through, I was sure I would find you at Ellen's house. And that we would catch Marty there. But I never thought you would be stupid enough to go inside to confront him. You can't do things like that. You are so lucky you weren't shot." My eyes suddenly filled with tears and ran down my cheeks. The entire ordeal had been terrifying and my whole body hurt. I simply couldn't handle a lecture from Matt right now. I buried my head into my blankets and sobbed. "Oh geeze, Sydney. I'm sorry. I didn't mean to make you cry. Honestly. I was just so worried and when I arrived at Ellen's and learned you were inside, I thought Marty might have killed you. Please stop crying." Matt practically begged, as he patted my hands and rubbed my arm to soothe me.

Looking up from the blankets, I fought to stop my blubbering. "I'm okay. I'm just emotional. It's been a heck of a couple of days. I think I'm just overwhelmed right now." I wiped the tears from my cheeks and attempted a smile. Matt smiled back, looking relieved that I had stopped crying. Maybe he wasn't as tough as I thought.

Matt stood up. "I'm sure you would like to see Ellen soon. She gave her statement already and explained what Marty planned to do with her, and what he said about Bob and Eddie. And once you are feeling better, we will have to get a statement from you, too. But for now, you need to rest." Matt started walking toward the door, then turned and walked back over to my bed. "I just have to ask you one question before I leave."

"Aright."

"I have figured out most of the puzzle, but before Ellen comes in, I just need to fill in a missing piece." I nodded for him to continue. "If you didn't get my message about Marty, then how did you know it was him?" I couldn't help but smile. I had been one ahead of him, and I bet that burned a bit.

"The button." Matt's head tilted and his whole forehead wrinkled as he tried to figure out what I meant, so I continued. "The button I saw on the barn floor near where Eddie was attacked. I knew I had seen it somewhere before, but just couldn't remember. Then I saw Marty at the fair. He came to see me because he was looking for Ellen. He was wearing his funky jacket again. The one with the wide collar. Have you seen him wearing it around town? Seems he is always wearing it, which I think is nutty, because it is definitely not stylish. I think it's hideous." Matt shook his head no. "Anyway, that's when I remembered."

"Remembered what?"

"I remembered it was Marty's jacket that had those buttons. I had never seen any like them before. Big, shiny silver and red buttons. When Marty was walking over to me, I noticed that one of his buttons was missing. One of the silver ones. That's when everything clicked, and I knew it was him that had attacked Eddie. I didn't know why yet, but I was sure it was him. And he was after Ellen." I paused for a moment.

"Of course! The button. We hadn't come up with anything on that yet." Pleased that I had solved the puzzle first, I nodded and smiled.

"Why didn't Ellen call the police right then, while she was at the fair and surrounded by people? It would have been so much safer" Of course it would have been safer, but hindsight is twenty-twenty, as they say. I was feeling frustrated at Matt's questioning.

"I realize now that staying at the fair would have been best, Matt. But I don't think either of us realized just how dangerous Marty was. I mean, yes, he had been trying to talk to her, and didn't take no for an answer. But we didn't know that Marty had anything to do with Bob's death, or with Eddie's attack. I didn't figure that out until after Ellen had already left the fairgrounds. Besides, Ellen planned to call the police once she got home. And I couldn't call you while Marty was standing right in front of me. I planned to call as soon as he left my booth, but then he spotted Ellen's car leaving the parking lot. Anyway, I had to go after him. I didn't get a chance to call. And like I already told you, my phone died, so I couldn't call anyone at all. I couldn't leave Ellen alone with Marty. Who knows what he planned to do with her? So, I snuck in the back door. And well, that's how I ended up at Ellen's. And you know the rest." I winced as I reached for my water. The meds must have been worn off because I could feel the pain returning. I was also getting tired. I leaned back against my pillow and closed my eyes.

"I'm going to go now. I'll send Ellen in. Do you need anything?"

"Ya, on your way out, can you tell the nurse I want some more of those pain meds?"

"Sure thing. I will come check on you tomorrow and follow up with anything else we need then. And Syd,"

I looked up at him, "if you ever do anything that crazy again, I might have to have you arrested." He winked and walked out the door.

Ellen came rushing in and hugged me hard. I let out a small squeak from the pain. "Oh dear, I'm so sorry." She jumped back away from me. "I wasn't thinking at all. You must be in such pain from the awful battle you had with that monster. How are you doing?"

"I'm going to be just fine. A little sore, but nothing that won't heal."

"How will I ever repay you for saving my life? I don't know what would have happened without you today. You know, I told the officer that took my statement that you were a hero. You really are a true hero, Sydney Jones."

"I couldn't very well leave you to fend for yourself in there now, could I? But I must admit, I had no idea Marty had a gun, or I might have taken a different approach. Next time." I joked. Ellen's face fell and her mouth dropped open. "I'm kidding Ellen. There will never be a next time for either of us. They will lock Marty away, and you will be safe to live your life." Suddenly, I felt lightheaded and woozy. "Ellen, I'm sorry to cut your visit short, but I need to close my eyes again for a bit."

"Of course. I will come and see you once they let you go home. Get some rest. And one last thing, Sydney."

I looked at her. “Nathan sends you well wishes and said to thank you for saving me.” With that, she slipped out the door. I was already drifting off.

Chapter 27

Harry's shoulder had healed, and he had got the all clear from his physiotherapist to bowl again. He was thrilled and so was the rest of our team. As I looked at the group of people gathered around the giant wooden table, I couldn't help but think back to a few short weeks ago, when they were all virtual strangers, and now I could call them my friends. We had just finished our Thursday night bowling game and now we waited to order our meals. This was a ritual I could fast get used to. Sandra leaned in and patted my arm affectionately.

"I can't believe how much you have improved in only a few short weeks, Sydney. You did so well bowling tonight. And to top it off, we now have Harry back on the team. The Wildcats might even win the trophy this year with our all-star team." Sandra gushed, and I blushed. Her husband, Harvey, sat at the other end of the table with his team. She waved over at him, and he winked and smiled at her. They acted like two young school kids, sending their secret love signals. Sandra's whole family had stopped by with lunch one day while I was stuck at home on the couch recovering. Her sons were both such fine young men and so thoughtful. While they were visiting me, the boys cut my lawn and took out my garbage. Sandra and her husband both helped inside. It was such a big help while I was on the mend. Although the doctor had only ordered me to stay off my feet for a few days, it sure seemed like much longer. Sandra had such a lovely family. And they might have saved my life that day they rescued me out of my wrecked car. My car had been written off, and I had bought a new one with the insurance money. It had all wheel drive, and I figured it was more suitable to living in Blueberry Falls. I loved my new car. New town, new house, new friends and a new car. I felt like my life from my old neighborhood was slowly being replaced. Except for Posh and Natasha, of course. They were irreplaceable.

Ellen sat beside me, to my right. She and I had become good friends in just the short time I had known her. I think the experience that we had gone through together probably strengthened our bond significantly. She also brought me meals and snacks on the days following my battle with Marty and his arrest. In fact, I had more homemade meals and goodies from the people in Blueberry Falls than I knew what to do with. My fridge and freezer were both full. I wouldn't have to cook for the next month.

Marty was charged with the murder of Bob Filmore, the attempted murder of Eddie Caldwell and me, and a slew of other charges, including kidnapping Ellen and me. Eddie, Ellen and I would all have to go to court to testify against him. I was looking forward to it. Ellen was not. She was nervous about having to face Marty. In fact, she was nervous about a lot of things lately, which I could totally relate to. I felt anxious since my breakup with Gerard. After waking from his coma, doctors released Eddie to heal at home. Doctors expected him to make a full recovery. I had heard through George that Ellen and their son Nathan had been spending a lot of time with Eddie at his farmhouse, helping to take care of things until he was fully back on his feet. Who knew? Maybe they would get back together again. Ellen said he was a different man since he wasn't drinking and carrying on anymore. She also said that Nathan and Eddie had always been close, so it was nice he got to spend so much time with his dad again.

After our food and drinks arrived, we all dug in heartily. Everyone was laughing and sharing stories. Harry stood up. "Hey guys. I just want to say a little toast to my dear old friend Bob, who we lost tragically." Everyone raised their glasses and cheered.

"To Bob!" we all said in chorus.

"And," Harry continued, "I want to thank my neighbor and friend Sydney for helping solve the crime. If Sydney hadn't helped, Marty might still be free, and Ellen might have been kidnapped and hidden somewhere in the woods at Marty's cabin." With that comment, Ellen turned and hugged me. Harry continued, "to Sydney!" Everyone cheered again. All the fuss and attention almost brought me to tears. I wasn't used to getting all this attention, but it sure felt good to belong. I was thankful that Harry had urged me to join the Thursday night bowling league at Riverbowl. Their motto really was true. "You belong here" I couldn't believe how much Blueberry Falls felt like home already and how many new friends I had made after only living here a few months.

For me, the whole string of events after finding Bob's body had rejuvenated some of my prior courage and curiosity. I had even quietly been looking into a private investigator course, which I had told to only Harry. I hadn't even mentioned it to Posh or Natalie yet. Harry said I would be good at being a P.I.. I doubted I would tell Matt anything about it at all, because I was sure he'd be irked. I also think I may have gotten another lecture about staying out of police business.

Since the whole Marty incident, I had gotten to know Matt a bit better, and as long as we stayed away from the topic of solving crimes as an amateur sleuth, we got along famously. He was a nice guy, even if he was a bit of a control freak. Me learning more about the topic of snooping and investigating crimes wouldn't be something he'd be happy about. Matt had been telling me to mind my own business the whole time I was trying to help find Bob's killer. Yet, in the end, it was me, not him, that had actually caught the killer and saved Ellen. Matt had brought flowers to my house while I recovered. And we spent a whole evening together on my couch watching movies when I first got home from the hospital. He had even made me dinner while I sat resting on my couch, and he acted like a real friend. And I must admit, I enjoyed spending time with him. He was handsome and thoughtful, well sometimes, when he's not in uniform anyway, and we seemed to get into the best conversations about so many interesting topics. But becoming a private investigator would be an issue, so I kept it to myself. I could just imagine what he would say to me. "*Stay out of police business, Sydney. Why can't you find something else to learn about? Not Private Investigator. You already have a good job at the bookstore.*" I understood Matt was just trying to keep me safe. But, whether or not I took the course, the decision was mine. I had spent most of my adult life trying to please my husband by being and doing what he wanted and look how that turned out. Gerard had decided I wasn't enough. And he threw away everything for a younger, apparently better woman. Well, I was single now. I was free to do as I chose. My daughter was all grown up and doing well in Ottawa. And I'd be darned if I was going to let someone dictate my life choices now. Besides, I was good at investigating. I was good at being snoopy and solving puzzles, and I loved it.

Laughter erupted at the other end of the table, bringing me out of my thoughts. George was telling jokes. Everyone thought he was hilarious. I didn't always agree, but his jokes were usually harmless. Even Angela had joined us after the game tonight. She and Harry were deep in conversation about something or other. Probably reminiscing about all their past shenanigans.

As I munched happily on my delicious honey garlic wings and sipped on my beer, I felt a tap on my shoulder. I turned to look, and Matt was standing there.

"Mind if I join you guys? I just finished a long shift and I'm starving."

"Of course, join us! Let me scootch on over a seat and you can park yourself right here beside Sydney?" Sandra winked at me as she slid into the empty seat beside her. Matt sat down and smiled at me.

"Can we get the man a beer, please?" Harry called out. "It's on me!"

"Sure thing, Mr. Lufkin. I'll be right over with one." The server was back in seconds with Matt's beer.

"Cheers," Matt turned to me, and I raised my bottle to his. I couldn't help but smile at him. Probably a big goofy grin, but whatever. I was happy he had joined us.

On the way home, my thoughts returned to the P.I. course. Tomorrow I would decide whether being a private investigator was in my future or not. Sydney Jones P.I.. I kind of liked that sound of that.

***

THE END

NOTE FROM AUTHOR

Although Blueberry Falls is a fictitious town placed in the Highlands, in rural Northern Ontario, Canada, Riverbowl is a real business, also located in a rural Ontario town.

The events and characters in the story are all fictitious, but the welcoming community and cozy atmosphere at Riverbowl really does exist. Also, the moto "You Belong Here" is a real part of Riverbowl.

So, if you ever find yourself in the Almaguin Highlands, in Ontario, looking for a cozy little place to go bowling, or if you love sports memorabilia, look them up. You won't be disappointed.

Grace Bowen is a voracious reader and a lover of all things bookish. She has loved reading mysteries ever since she was a young girl, quickly devouring books such as the Nancy Drew Mysteries, The Secret Seven and The Famous Five Series. Grace's love of mystery novels has continued into adulthood, and she continues reading as much as possible. Now Grace writes mystery novels for others to enjoy.

Grace lives on a farm in rural Canada, where she enjoys spending her time with her family and her animals, surrounded by nature.

Grace Bowen BOOKS

Manufactured by Amazon.ca
Bolton, ON

45612379R00136